KAITLY

Kaitlyn A. Potts

THE DANGERS

A FAMILY OF SPIES

outskirts
press

The Dangers
A Family of Spies
All Rights Reserved.
Copyright © 2018 Kaitlyn A. Potts
v2.0

This is a work of fiction. The events and characters described herein are imaginary and are not intended to refer to specific places or living persons. The opinions expressed in this manuscript are solely the opinions of the author and do not represent the opinions or thoughts of the publisher. The author has represented and warranted full ownership and/or legal right to publish all the materials in this book.

This book may not be reproduced, transmitted, or stored in whole or in part by any means, including graphic, electronic, or mechanical without the express written consent of the publisher except in the case of brief quotations embodied in critical articles and reviews.

Outskirts Press, Inc.
http://www.outskirtspress.com

ISBN: 978-1-4787-9526-1

Cover Photo © 2018 gettyimages.com. All rights reserved - used with permission.

Outskirts Press and the "OP" logo are trademarks belonging to Outskirts Press, Inc.

PRINTED IN THE UNITED STATES OF AMERICA

1

WHEN THE TIME IS RIGHT

It was 10:30 in the morning when Lucy and Charles Danger were making their daily rounds for the agency. The Dangers worked for a top-secret organization called GUARD, the Guided Universal Agency Restriction Department. They were professional spies, specializing in going undercover and giving their clients first-class, undetectable protection. GUARD has over 1.3 million locations around the world, including training facilities for the children of their agents.

When a couple becomes GUARD secret agents, they are required to sign a contract regarding the future of their children. The adult agents inform their children about GUARD and their chosen profession when the kids are deemed old enough to grasp the idea of exactly what they are involved in. This helps to ensure that the organization always has a future supply of agents. Then the kids are sent to a top-secret training facility for extensive, specialized, and dangerous spy training.

The time had finally arrived for Lucy and Charles Danger to enlighten their children about GUARD. They had been looking forward to and preparing for this day with much anticipation for many years. Laci and Brady, their twin children, were now old enough to comprehend the nature of their secret work. Watching the twins grow up through the years and knowing that this day would arrive was so very exciting for Lucy and Charles. Even so, they were apprehensive about what the twins would think when they shared with them their life and activities of being secret agents.

So many questions raced through their heads as they thought about the future of Laci and Brady.

How would they do in the spy training program?

What would be their strengths and weaknesses?

What missions would they be assigned to?

Would they get to work together as a team, or would they go solo, or be assigned to another partner?

What parts of the world would they get to see?

Would they someday get an opportunity to save the world?

They thought about how blessed they were to be able to give their children such an exciting and adventurous lifestyle. So few are chosen. Lucy and Charles Danger were pretty proud parents.

Now that you know the beginning of the story let me give you some more details about the Danger children.

Thirteen-year-old fraternal twins Laci and Brady Danger had just arrived home from school. The twins had bright blond hair, but Brady had spiked his hair up, and Laci usually wore her hair in a ponytail. Both kids had playful, friendly freckles on their faces and deep blue eyes.

Laci took off her backpack full of books and gently laid it down on a shelf next to the door. Just then, she heard a loud thump from upstairs.

"Brady?"

"Uh-huh."

"What was that?"

Brady looked behind him. In his hurry to start up his computer, he must have dropped his backpack. It was Friday, and they were so happy that school was out for summer break.

"Um, I dropped my backpack . . ." he said guiltily.

Laci rolled her eyes. You see, Brady was always dropping

things as he rushed home. However, this time, it was different. There would be no school the next day, so she didn't need to remind him to pick up his things.

Laci sighed. "Just, be careful with your stuff, Brady."

Silence filled the room, but Laci could still hear the *thump-a-dee-thump-thump* of Brady's feet from upstairs.

"Laci!" Brady shouted.

"What?" she responded.

"Come play on the Xbox with me. I can put on *Minecraft*, or *Disney Infinity*, or *Skylanders*, or—"

"OK, OK, I get it; just let me think. You're speaking way too fast for me to hear. Hmm . . ."

Laci thought for a minute and realized that she hadn't spent much quality time with her brother, and she hadn't gotten to play *Minecraft* lately either. Meanwhile, Brady was getting impatient.

"So?" he asked. "You gonna play or not?"

"OK, OK, I'm coming!" Laci shouted back.

She ran up the stairs and played on the Xbox until their eyes hurt. After playing all of the games that Brady had, they were reminded of when they were about eight years old.

Back then, neither Laci nor Brady had many worries in their life. No pressure, many good friends and there was definitely NO bullying.

"That was fun," he said.

"Yeah, it was! I haven't had that much fun on the Xbox in a long time. Reminds me of the good ol' days . . ."

Suddenly, they heard the sound of keys, and then the front door swung open.

It must be Mom and Dad, they thought.

The two children looked at each other, nodded, and smiled. Since they were twins, they had a special intuitive bond and usually knew what the other was thinking. They ran down the stairs, hugged, and greeted their parents.

Charles and Lucy were happy to see their kiddos and

answered questions about their day, but it was almost time to reveal the truth about their chosen profession. For the past thirteen years of their lives, the kids were told that their parents were attorneys. Soon, their secret agent undercover lifestyle would be exposed. They could wait no longer. After dinner, they had to tell the kids. You see, the next day, the kids would be loaded into an unmarked van and driven to a training camp in some obscure location near Dallas, Texas. So they summoned the kids into the living room and prepared to reveal their secret life.

"So, what's so important, Mom?" Laci was a little concerned. The last time they had a family meeting, it was about moving from Maryland to New York. Laci had no idea why they had to move and thought their lives were perfect in Maryland.

"We need to tell you something," Lucy said. "Something we should have told you long ago but didn't. For the past thirteen years of your life, we have been keeping a big secret from you and the rest of the world too. We are not who you think we are. We—"

"You're not our real parents?" Brady shouted. He looked panicked and started to race around the room like a balloon that had just lost its air. Laci quickly realized by the look on her mom's face that it was not true. She gave Brady what they laughingly refer to as the "Sister Stink Eye" look. He quickly got her message and sat back down.

"We are not lawyers. We-we are secret agents. We work for an organization called GUARD. We know this is a shock to you and hard to process, but trust us, you will soon understand completely.

"What we have told you is TOP SECRET. You cannot discuss this with anyone, not even your best friends. You are to trust *no one* with this information," Lucy finished with a stern look.

Laci and Brady were shocked. They looked at each other, then their parents, then back at each other.

"You're joking, right? You guys aren't really secret agents,"

THE DANGERS

Laci said nervously. She began to realize that her world was about to change dramatically.

"We aren't kidding," Lucy said with a soft tenderness that only a loving mother could convey to her child. "This is the truth. We hope you are not upset with us."

Laci looked at Brady.

"No, of course not. We understand why you couldn't tell us. It was to protect us, right?"

"Yes, it was for your own good and safety. But now that you know about the agency, we have some more information for you," Charles continued.

"You both get to join GUARD and begin some very special training to become Secret Agents." The kids were about to explode with excitement.

"So, we get to go on missions, fight crime, work in a secret agency, be spies, AND GET COOL GADGETS?" Brady squealed like a pig stuck in a gate.

Brady was a computer genius and loved any sort of cool gadgets, toys, and anything that had to do with a remote control. He could program a computer with his hands tied behind his back. REALLY! Once, for show-and-tell at school, he programmed a computer with his nose. And although it was a little strange, it did prove how good he is with computers.

"Yes, in time, Brady, but first, you have to be fully trained in espionage," his father said.

"Cool! So when do we start?" Laci asked. She was as eager as her brother to become a secret agent. She was very athletic, secretive, and almost intuitively liked to spy on what her parents got her for her birthday and Christmas. She could always figure out what her gift was.

"Well, that's just the thing . . ." Lucy answered. "You're leaving . . . tomorrow."

"WHAT?" the kids exclaimed. "Where are we going?" Laci asked. She needed to prepare for wherever their destination was.

"Dallas," Charles said. "Dallas, Texas."

"That's why you need to go and pack your bags before your transportation gets here in the morning," their mother continued.

The kids looked at each other a bit worried about the trip ahead. Then, they ran upstairs to pack their things and get ready for the day ahead of them.

"Mom," Laci asked, "how many days will we be gone? And where will we stay?"

"You will be gone for about a year, and you will live in dorms at the academy," her mom answered.

Laci heard a slight mumbling voice coming from Brady's room.

"Great, back to school again," he groaned.

"Yeah, but instead of school for the average kid, we get to go to a school for spies and secret agents," Laci said, peeking around the corner of Brady's door. "And, hey, remember, there will be a bunch of other kids just like us at that academy."

"Yeah, I guess you're right," Brady smiled. He started to brush back his spiky hair as if it was an annoyance. "Maybe we can get cool uniforms too."

He crammed all of his things into two suitcases and was ready to go.

Laci went back to work on her packing, and by 10:00 p.m., their rooms were basically packed up in suitcases.

Tomorrow, they would embark upon the adventure of a lifetime. An adventure that most kids only see in movies or read about in books. As you will soon see, their adventure will take Laci and Brady on many exciting twists and turns.

As Sherlock Holmes would say . . . "Let the games begin."

2

A Long Way from Home

The warm light of the morning sun crept through Laci's bedroom window and warmed her face. As she peeked open her eyes, she lay startled because most of the things in her bedroom had disappeared. Then she remembered. Her parents are secret agents, and that morning, she and Brady were going to travel to Dallas, Texas, for a year of training to be secret agents. She jumped out of bed, got dressed, gathered her luggage, and carried it downstairs.

"Brady," she whispered. "Brady, are you awake?"

He turned around in his bed and saw his sister's head peeking out from behind the door.

"Brady?" she repeated. He grinned.

"Um . . . What if I say no?"

"Brady, come on! We have to get ready for our trip to Dallas."

"What trip?"

Laci was getting annoyed with Brady.

"Cool spy stuff, remember?"

"OH YEAH!" He jumped out of bed and quickly put on his clothes.

"Well, don't just stand there. We need to get going if we're going to make it to the airport on time," he said to Laci.

Lucy Danger had prepared a delicious breakfast for the kids. The family sat around the breakfast table, and the parents exchanged a few last-minute instructions for their kiddos. This was the last meal they would share with their kids for many months to come.

An unmarked van drove up in front of the Dangers' house, and as they hugged and said their good-byes, Charles offered one last piece of advice for his kids.

He had for each of the children a brand-new Bible. The Dangers had taken the kids to church and taught them the importance of God in their life.

"You kids know the importance of prayer, Bible study, and God in your life. Take these Bibles and continue to apply the principles herein to your lives and God will bless you," Charles said as he handed them their new Bibles.

About an hour later, Brady and Laci arrived at the airport. Security guards armed with machine guns and wearing bulletproof vests were standing at the boarding gate. Soon, they would all board a private jet and be escorted to an obscure landing facility somewhere around Dallas, Texas.

"Laci," Lucy said. She had a serious look on her face. She took hold of her daughter and looked straight into her deep blue eyes. "Promise me that you will take good care of your brother. Make sure you have each other's backs in your new home for a year, okay?"

Laci looked at her mom; then she looked at Brady. He was hugging Dad. Then she looked back at her mom.

"I will, Mom," she said. Tears began to trickle down her mom's cheeks as they hugged each other ever so tightly.

"I'll miss you," Laci said.

"I will miss you too, honey." Lucy looked at her daughter, then released her and let her go.

Laci turned toward her dad and hugged him tightly. "I'll miss you so much, Dad," she said.

"I will miss you too, sweetie," he said as he let go of her.

THE DANGERS

"Remember, even when things get tough, keep trying and don't give up. Also, you know you can call us at any time, twenty-four-seven, and we will come running."

Laci smiled at her dad. She always loved to hear his advice. Then she turned toward her brother.

Just then, one of the guards walked up.

"Laci and Brady Danger, I am here to inform you that your private plane will be leaving soon. Are you ready to begin your journey?" he asked them.

Laci looked at Brady, and he looked at her. They nodded affirmatively at the same time.

"What's your name?" Laci asked the guard.

"Uh . . . um . . ." He leaned closer to them, then looked from one side to the other. "Joe," he whispered. "My name is Joe."

"Well, Joe," Laci smiled, "you bet; we are ready."

Joe stood up and gestured at the gateway toward the plane. Laci and Brady took their seats on the plane and began their three-hour flight to Spy School.

Upon arriving, they stepped out of the airplane and climbed into a limo. Brady looked surprised at how huge Love Field Airport was.

"Wow! I know I've never been to Dallas before, but I thought Texas was all cowboys and horses. It turns out it's not that different from most cities in New York," he said.

"Yeah, you're right; it's not that different. Kind of reminds me of home," Laci chimed in.

In their excitement, she had not thought about being away from home for so long. It was their first time away from home and family. She shot a quick glance at her brother, and they began to cry.

"You OK?" she asked.

Brady wiped his eyes. "Yeah, I'm OK," he said in a low, crackling voice.

Laci looked around for something to cheer her brother up. She knocked on the window that was behind the driver's seat, and Joe rolled down the window. He was holding a Coke in his hand.

"Use this," he said. "Trust me, it works."

Laci smiled and grabbed the Coke through the open window. She could see Joe's grinning face in the mirror. He rolled up the window, and Laci turned around to face her brother.

"Hey . . ." she said.

"Hey," he said sadly and continued to stare out the window.

"Come on, Brady! Cheer up! I have a Coke for you."

Brady looked up with a little smile on his face. "Thanks," he said. "I'll be OK. But can you give me the Coke already? I'm parched." Laci laughed and handed him the drink.

Before long, they arrived at the academy. Brady thought he had died and gone to heaven.

"WOW! This place looks awesome."

"It consists of advanced technology," Joe said. "Very advanced technology and I think y'all will be highly impressed, especially you, Brady." Brady looked like he was going to burst with excitement.

Laci was a little perplexed. "If I take a step back, everyone and this huge dome-shaped training facility disappears."

"That's a cloaking device. You see, as we walk, the parts behind us disappear to the naked eye. So, even though this facility is already in a remote part of the county, we don't want any tourists accidentally stumbling upon it."

Joe walked them inside the academy in search of their dorms.

"Here is your dorm, Laci," Joe said. "You have two roommates, Christy Haul and Abby Swing. Brady, you are down the hall in the boys' dorms."

Laci was curious about who was going to be rooming with her bro, just in case of an emergency.

"Um, Joe, what room is Brady's, and who will he be staying with?" she asked.

"Brady will be in room 346, and his roommates are Andrew

Brach and David Cue. Remember that your roommates are just like you, and this is also their first day here," he said.

"Yes, sir," Brady and Laci answered.

"Here are your schedules, a map of the academy, calendars, and lunch menus. The introduction of the teachers and trainers will take place at 6:00 tonight. Don't be late! Okay, now I'll take Brady to his dorm, and you should get settled into your new home, Miss Laci," Joe continued.

Laci looked at her brother, and he looked at her. *Promise me you won't do anything dumb. Remember, I won't be there to put Humpty Dumpty back together again,* she thought. Her brother seemed to know what she was thinking intuitively.

"I'll be fine, Laci. I'm the same age as you are; I can take care of myself." Brady seemed to be stepping up to the plate with more confidence than ever before. He was already becoming a force to deal with.

"I know . . . I just don't want that blond, spiky hair to get you in trouble again," she teased.

Laci thought back to when Brady was six years old and began to take an interest in spiky hairstyles. She reminded him when he spiked his hair with so much gel that his hair looked like pine needles. He accidentally kept poking people with that spiked hair until his dad grounded him from using hair gel for a week.

"Oh, come on; that was only once and a long time ago," he said. Laci smiled.

"I know, I'm just teasing you," she said as she ruffled her brother's spiky hair.

Brady and Joe began walking toward the boys' dorms. Laci watched them turn the corner until she could see them no longer. She took a deep breath, then turned the doorknob of the door leading into her new home.

"Here we go," she told herself as she grabbed her luggage and opened the door.

3

NEW SCHOOL AND NEW FRIENDS

Laci looked around her new headquarters. The walls were painted pink with a large full-view window half surrounding the room and overlooking the academy gardens. There were three beds with white drawers installed at the foot of each one. Three vanities with mirrors lined one wall.

She realized that her two roommates were checking her out. One girl was holding a dirty and slightly damaged soccer ball. She had short brown hair and hazel-blue eyes. The other roommate was preoccupied with some object, but Laci could not determine what it was. Her appearance was very similar to Laci's. She was about the same age as Laci, and like Laci, she also had blond hair and pretty blue eyes. Both girls were staring at Laci.

"Um . . . Hi. I'm Laci, and I believe I'm your new roomie." Laci looked at them and smiled sheepishly. The girl with the long blond hair smiled kindly at Laci.

"Hi, Laci, I'm Abby Swing, and this is my best friend Christy Haul," she said.

Christy Haul looked up from her old, scratched and well used soccer ball. "Hi," Christy said cheerfully.

Laci put her luggage on her bed and began to unpack. When she was about halfway finished putting away her things, she

THE DANGERS

looked up and saw Christy working on her laptop with Abby and her old soccer ball right by her side. Laci noticed that Abby would look at the soccer ball, then the laptop, the soccer ball, then the laptop, etc. She couldn't help but wonder what the deal was with that ridiculous soccer ball.

"Pardon me for asking, Christy, but why do you seem to be in love with that old soccer ball?"

Christy looked at Laci and grinned. "I'm glad you asked," she said.

"This old soccer ball is a reminder to Christy and me about how we developed such a strong bond with each other," said Abby with a smile.

"You see, when we were about six years old," Christy continued, "we played on the same soccer team. We lost the first game of the season when the other team made a goal with only a few seconds left. We were crushed and so disappointed. It was a real heartbreaker, to be so close to winning and come up short. After that, we kept losing and losing, over and over again."

"But one day," Abby continued the story, "I went on a family vacation for a week in Colorado to visit my Aunt Harriett and Uncle Doug. While I was gone, my team won both games. I was so happy to know that they had finally won a couple of games." But then Abby's smile turned into a sad frown.

"But when I rejoined my team to play the next game, some of my teammates confronted me and wanted to know why I was back from Colorado. I told them it was just a family trip and that I wasn't moving there. The kids told me that I was bad luck to the team, and they did not want me to play on the team anymore. I was shocked that they would say such a hurtful thing over a soccer game, but I was determined to play anyway."

Christy looked at Laci and continued the story. "Right when the game was about to end, Abby stole the ball. In the confusion of everyone around her going for the ball, Abby saw daylight for the goal and took off. It was beautifully and gracefully done. She left the pack of kids, raced ahead of them all, sped down the field, and kicked the ball perfectly into the goal. She raised her hands and shouted triumphantly. But for some reason, the rest of the team was not clapping or cheering. You see, Abby had kicked the soccer ball into the wrong goal and scored for the other team. How embarrassed she was. Her team lost the game. She went, in one split second, from hero to zero. Her teammates were so upset with her.

I shielded and hugged her to give her protection from the other angry teammates. They told her that she was bad luck and had to leave the team and never play soccer again.

I was so mad at our teammates for being mean to Abby. I took the team's 'lucky' soccer ball and went to the nearest mud puddle. In my madness, I dunked that ball in the mud. Then I washed off a place on the ball, took out my Sharpie pen, and wrote this on the ball: *'Christy and Abby, best friends forever, together.'* Then I gave that soccer ball to Abby, took her hand in mine, and we walked off the field together. We were the winners that day because we became wonderful friends as a result of a dumb old soccer game and some foolish teammates."

"WOW." Laci had never heard such a bold act of friendship in her life. The story touched her. "You guys are really true best friends."

"This is the same ball," Christy said as she proudly held it up for Laci to see. "It's a good reminder of how lemons become lemonade." They all laughed.

"Wow," Laci said again as she started to unpack once more. "What a story. Someone should put that in a book someday."

She looked at her watch, and her eyes grew big.

"GIRLS," she yelled, "WE'RE GOING TO BE LATE FOR THE PRESENTATION!" She grabbed her map of the academy and threw open the door. All three girls ran down the hall to the community center and took their seats.

Laci looked around for some sign of her brother. *Nothing ... Where could he be?* she thought. Then, she suddenly caught sight of his spiky blond hair in the front row. He was safe and sitting beside two other boys.

A woman's voice sounded over the microphone. The woman looked firm but friendly, and without a moment's hesitation, she started the presentation.

"Hello, students, I am Agent Huffman. Since I am your adviser and teacher, you may simply call me Miss Huffman. During this year, you will be trained by professionals to become secret agents like your parents. It will not be all work and no play. We will arrange for you to go into the city, explore the stores, and enjoy a movie from time to time. However, for your own protection, you will be escorted by security guards.

"The academy will provide all of the gadgets, spy gear, arms, ammunition, and other specialty items that you will need for your training. Don't worry, girls, there is a spa and lounging area for you to hang out. The boys will get a lounge area also, along with an arcade equipped with some high-tech gaming systems. There is also a bedtime curfew requirement."

All of the kids groaned, and some rolled their eyes. "Be careful with all that groaning. I can take back independence time . . ." Miss Huffman threatened. Then all of the kids got quiet.

"Thank you. Your bedtime curfew is 9:30. If you are not in bed, a security guard will find you, and punishment will be issued. This academy has high standards, and every one of you will be expected to be on your best behavior for the entire time you are here. Understand?"

The crowd nodded their heads.

"Good. I wish you the best as you begin your training. Thank you and good night."

The students went back to their rooms and got ready for bed. Laci, Christy, and Abby continued to get acquainted with each other by telling stories of their lives, friendships, and scary moments that they had experienced. Quickly, they became a trio of best friends forever.

When Laci went to bed for the night, she was happy and hoped that Brady was happy too. She knew it was going to be a long and grueling year but an exciting one. She was glad her new roommates were so terrific.

4

Let's Do It!

It was 8:00 in the morning at the academy, and all the students were heading toward their classes. Laci, Abby, and Christy's first class was called Spy 101, and they were eager to get started.

"The agility field is my kind of place to be," Christy told them. She was really excited.

"Welcome to your first class, boys and girls," Miss Huffman said. "Today, in Spy 101, you will be taught agility. We have set up an obstacle course to test your stealth, flexibility, speed, and quick thinking. We will test you one at a time. Let's start with . . ." She looked at her clipboard and passed a pen over the names of the kids that stood in front of her. "Brady Danger, you will start us off."

"Ahh, man, I wanted to go first," Christy pouted.

Laci looked down the row of kids, and sure enough, Brady was standing at the end of the line. His palms were sweating. He was not too happy about being the first person to do this. He swallowed hard and walked up to the teacher.

"Where should I begin, Miss Huffman?" he asked nervously. Miss Huffman smiled and pointed over to a red flag.

"You will start over there and maneuver your way through a tunnel. Then you will go through a vent to test your flexibility.

You will then be timed to see how fleet of foot you are. Lastly, you will be given a test to see how quickly you think. I cannot tell you what that test consists of," said Miss Huffman.

Brady walked over to the red flag and mentally prepared himself for whatever he would face next. Miss Huffman blew her whistle.

"GO!" she yelled.

Brady bolted out of the starting position. He was lightning fast, and all you could see was a blur of black. He climbed his way through the tunnel, then made his way to the vent. Because of his small compact body, he easily maneuvered his way through the vent. Countless times in his younger years, he had crawled into tiny spaces to hide from people whom he did not want to see. He crawled out of the vent and quickly made his way to the speed portion of the test. He appeared on some type of track, and it went on and on for what seemed to be forever.

It was a bright sunny day, and Brady could feel the warm sun on his back and shoulders. Just then, he saw a huge shadow in front of him, and the warm sun disappeared.

What was that? How was he going to escape? Brady ran as fast as his legs would go until he found himself trapped in a small room with an open entry door. He carefully peeped through the door. What he saw was incredible. It was a huge dinosaur outside the door. He quickly slammed the door shut, locked it, and threw his body against it.

There was a tiny table by the door. On top of it was a note that said, "*You are trapped. You must discover a way out before the T. Rex stomps down the door and eats you. You have a hammer, a sword, and a sharp knife. Time is running out.*"

Brady put the note back on the table and studied what he was given to work with.

Then he heard a muffled sound. As he turned around, he saw two pairs of glowing red eyes in the corner of the room.

What next? he thought. *Be calm, don't panic. You can do this.*

THE DANGERS

In that split second, he came up with an idea. *Since the room is made of wood . . .* He pressed his hand on one of the room walls, and it moved just a little. *Since the room is made of unstable wood . . .* he thought, *I'll use the hammer to pry the boards on the wall and break out of here.*

Then he heard screeching noises from the corners of the room and they were getting louder and louder. He turned just in time to see flying robots with fiery red eyes hovering just above his head.

He quickly raised the hammer and began to pry open the wooden planks. It worked. He broke off one piece of wood, slipped through it, and hastily left the T. Rex, the flying robots, and that little shack far behind. He ran as fast as he could and didn't look back until he had successfully finished the course.

"Wow! That was fun," Brady said as he panted for air from being out of breath.

Joe took Brady to the shower room to calm him down. He thought his new buddy was a little too worked up after his first day of training.

On that day, Brady received an A+ on the agility course. He was one happy camper. *Now, this is my kind of school,* he thought.

All of the other kids took their turns on the course, and they all received pretty good grades. Laci got an A+ like her brother, and so did Christy and Abby. When the class had ended, Laci ran up to her brother and gave him a big hug.

"Nice job on the course today, bro. You were great," she exclaimed.

"Thanks, Laci, you were pretty good yourself," he said with a big smile.

"So, how have you been doing with your new buddies, Andrew and David?" she asked.

"We've been doing great. Last night, Andrew was playing with the Taser watch and accidentally shocked himself. It was so funny. The three of us laughed for hours. Joe even had to come and remind us that it was time to go to bed and stop laughing." Brady had to keep from laughing out loud in front of everybody there.

Then a brown-haired boy motioned for Brady to come over.

"Gotta go. That's Andrew. Nice meeting up with you, sis." Brady ran up to a tall boy with brown hair and freckles. Another shorter boy with caramel, shaggy hair joined them. They all ran back inside to their next class.

Christy and Abby joined Laci. "OK, our next class is Gadgets and Gear, so we better get a move on," Abby told them.

The girls bolted into the building and walked down the hall to their next class. The room was full of what seemed like ordinary items on one side of the room, and on the other side were jet packs, cool guns, and even a rocket prototype.

Abby looked like she was in heaven. "Now, *this* is my kind of class."

"Abby has a knack for advanced technology," Christy informed Laci. "And I have a knack for jet packs."

Laci was lost in the maze of high-tech. She knew Abby had found her niche in the technology field, her brother and Christy in agility, but she still hadn't found where she would excel. She wanted to find her purpose in the academy. *I wonder if they have a stealth class. That would definitely be my place*, she thought.

"Hello, there, students," said a tall, slim man in a lab coat. "I am Professor Zorkoff. I am responsible for creating all of the gadgets for the agents of GUARD. I will be your teacher for the upcoming year. Today, you will be given your own personal gadgets and be instructed on their purpose and usage."

YES, Abby thought.

"I can see that some of you are pretty excited," Professor Zorkoff said as he glanced over in Abby's direction. "So let's begin."

He set down multiple gadgets on two glowing blue tables.

"Every one of you must have at least a pair of spy glasses, either a comb Taser, or a lip gloss Taser, a stealth suit of your choosing, a jet pack of your choice, a grappling hook backpack, a utility belt, hologram cameras, diversion steam bombs, and a disguise gadget."

Abby, Christy, and the other students raced to the tables. Laci cautiously stepped toward a utility belt. It was black and outlined in pink. She grabbed it and put it around her waist. Next, she saw the Tasers. She grabbed a lip gloss Taser and went toward the next gadget. It looked like square buttons and was labeled "Cloaking Devices." She grabbed one and stuck it on her utility belt. Then, she grabbed a jet pack and headed toward the "uniform" center of the lab. Everybody was already there with their cool gadgets. She walked up to Abby and Christy and noticed that Abby wore a black belt with a light blue outline, and Christy's belt had a purple outline.

"Cool belts, ladies," she told them.

"You too, Laci," Christy said with a smile. They walked into a room that had spy outfits on display all around the wall.

"Here, you will choose an outfit that suits you," the professor said. "These outfits will be your uniforms for the rest of the year. So, make sure they are flexible and comfortable. When you choose the one you want, simply walk into the capsule. A mist will cover you. Once the mist dissolves, just step back out of the capsule. Oh, and make sure before you go into the capsule to take off your utility belts."

Laci looked around for just the right one. Then she saw a black outfit with a purple tint. It was outlined in pink. She took off her utility belt and walked inside the capsule. A thick cloud of mist covered her and filled the capsule. The next thing she knew, her new outfit was comfortable on her body. She walked out of the capsule and put her utility belt back on. She observed that Abby was wearing a black outfit with a dark blue tint and blue outlining. She wore a dark blue leather jacket that went down to her rib cage. Christy's outfit looked similar to Laci's. It was black with a dark purple tint and a purple outline. She was also wearing a dark purple leather jacket, just like Abby's.

"Where did you find the jackets?" Laci asked.

"Over on the other side of the room," Christy said. "You get to customize your own."

"AWESOME," remarked Laci.

When they finished selecting their uniforms, Professor Zorkoff dismissed them from class, along with all the other students.

"I think we are going to head down to the spa. Would you care to join us?" Christy asked.

"Thanks, I'll catch up in a bit. I'm going to grab my jacket; then I'll meet you at the spa."

"OK, just remember to stop by the room and get your map. We don't know where the spa is," Abby reminded her.

"I will."

And with that, Abby and Christy left the room.

Laci went to the jacket customizer to make a dark magenta jacket. When finished, she made her way back to the room, took off her utility belt, and placed it on the bed. Then, she grabbed the map and headed down the hall to the spa.

5

LURKING SHADOWS

Two months had already passed. Being away from home was the hardest part for Laci and Brady. During the day, the academy kept their bodies and minds occupied with all sorts of instructions and training. But the night was the hard part.

Bedtime at home meant a Bible verse from Dad, accompanied by some explanation of what it meant, then some examples of how the kids could apply the biblical principles to their daily lives. After Dad gave hugs, I love yous, and kisses, Mom followed up by tucking them in bed, and then more hugs, I love yous, and kisses. Oh, how they missed that nightly ritual. But the nighttime blues were getting better now. At least, they were no longer crying themselves to sleep.

By now, some of the trainees had already bombed out and had to be sent home until another time. In some cases, the kids were not mentally ready, and in other cases, they were not physically adept. Brady and Laci had proven themselves to be highly competent in both areas and were exceptionally gifted, both mentally and physically.

On this day, Brady and his roommates were leaving their Gadgets 101 class and were headed to Computer Programming. When they entered the class, they noticed long computer screens lining all of the walls. Each screen had specific information on it. The boys also noticed different robot prototype models. Everything in the room was high-tech. Brady was having the time of his life learning how each item was programmed and how to make it function.

"This is awesome, bros," Andrew exclaimed. He was a big tech fan also and had a lot in common with Brady. For example, they both had spiky hair, except Andrew's hair was brown. They both loved high-tech, and they liked doing a lot of the same activities.

"Totally radical, dude," Brady exclaimed. He was trying to sound and be as cool as his new roommates. "I wonder if this has a 100-zettabyte server. That would be AWESOME."

"I don't know, dude," Andrew said. He brushed back his brown hair out of his face in order to look older and more distinguished. "This server can't possibly hold more than 10 zettabytes of power," he said, standing tall and playing around like he was the professor. The other boys in the class stared at him, looked at each other, and then burst into laughter.

"Wow, Andrew, that was hilarious," David exclaimed. The class could not stop laughing until Professor Zorkoff entered. Then Andrew took his seat and silence filled the room.

"It is all good to have fun and games, boys, but not around expensive and high-tech computers," said the professor. "And I'll have you know, young man, we do have a 100-zettabyte server. You have good skills, I see. Good job, good job, indeed."

Brady looked at Andrew and smiled as if to say, "I told you so."

"Whatever, dude," Andrew grinned back at Brady.

When Brady first met his roommates, Andrew and David, he knew they would all be good friends. Andrew had an outgoing personality and never met a stranger. He communicated well and loved to make people laugh.

David was more of the quiet, studious type. He didn't

speak very often, but when he did, everyone paid close attention because what he said was important. David was very good at agility, stealth, and high-tech gadgets. David's personality was very similar to Laci's. Brady thought about his sister and wondered how she was doing at the academy.

He turned on a computer and began his work. Suddenly, he saw the flash of a shadowy figure in the corner of his eye. As he turned to see what it was, the dark figure disappeared. There was nothing. How strange. Was he seeing things, or had something really been there? He became haunted by the feeling that someone or something was watching him.

Brady leaned over and whispered to Andrew and David, "Hey, do you guys feel like we're being watched?"

"Yes," Andrew said as he looked back at David. "I feel it too, and I don't like it."

David chimed in and shook his head. "Neither do I, not one little bit."

"We can't just get up from class and search the premises for a ghost. We need a plan. Got any ideas?" Andrew said.

"Is there some way that we might convince the professor to dismiss us?" Brady asked, "Then we could look for some clues."

Andrew dreamed up the perfect scheme. In just a few minutes, they strolled up to the professor and put their plan into action.

"Um, Professor," Andrew said and began wobbling a little as he walked up to the instructor. Then he put his hand up to his mouth and held his breath.

"I think I'm going to be sick," he told the professor. Then Brady walked up next to Andrew and did the same thing.

"Me too."

Andrew quickly grabbed his duffle bag, stuck his head inside, and made noises like he was throwing up. Brady did the same thing, and then David. Soon, the professor got their message.

"You three are dismissed. Go to your dorm, go to the bathroom—go anywhere but don't stay here."

That was just what they wanted. The boys ran out the door, into the hall, and to their lockers. At this time of day, the halls were empty, and everything was silent. The boys leaned against the lockers and took a moment to catch their breath. Everyone else was either having free time, were in their dorms, or in class.

Andrew looked at his watch. "Okay, we only have about thirty minutes to investigate. After that, it will be lunchtime, and we'll have to be there for roll call and lunch."

They walked down the hall looking for clues of some mysterious ghostly image that Brady had caught a glimpse of. Suddenly, they heard footsteps from behind. They stopped dead in their tracks. Without looking back, they could tell that the footsteps were getting closer and closer and closer. Finally, Brady jerked Andrew and David behind a nearby locker.

"Shush," he whispered. He peeked out from behind the locker, but whoever or whatever it was, had disappeared.

"They must have turned a corner . . ." Brady said, relieved but apprehensive about who it might have been. He ducked back behind the locker.

"Do you think that might have been our mystery person?" Andrew asked.

"Yeah, probably so. All of the staff members and professors are teaching students. I don't think any of them would be roaming around the academy at eleven thirty. It's not even lunchtime yet," Brady said.

Something was going on. Surely, they weren't the only ones in the school who had noticed something suspicious. What if it was someone who was spying on the academy? Or what if they were specifically targeting Brady, Andrew, and David? But why? They were just trainees. Brady began to be a little more concerned. Unanswered questions filled his mind. Were they in trouble? Was this some type of test? Was the academy staff in on it?

The bell rang for lunch; their investigation was over for now. Brady thought of a way to get more help to search for this mysterious shadow. How about enlisting Laci and her new friends to help? Surely they too have seen some weird activity around the academy. At lunch, he discussed with the boys how they could get the girls to join in on the investigation.

"DUDE, whoa, back up. You have a *sister?*" Andrew said, surprised.

"Yeah, so?"

"HOW COME YOU'VE NEVER TOLD ME THIS?"

"I-uh-I don't know. Why? Is that important?"

Andrew leaned toward him and whispered, "Is she pretty?"

Brady was stunned and looked at Andrew with one fist raised. Settling himself, he looked around the lunchroom for the girls. Soon, he found Laci's blond hair and blue eyes peek out from the crowd of students. He stood up and walked toward her. About halfway through the lunchroom, he felt like he was being watched. He stopped walking and looked around the room and found out that the *whole cafeteria* was staring at him. He felt like a fish in a bowl. Why was everybody staring at him? He looked down to see if anything was on him. Nothing was there . . . What was going on? He turned around and caught a glimpse of Andrew and David frantically motioning him to come back. Brady practically ran toward them, and as soon as he sat back down, everybody went back to eating their lunch.

"What was that all about?" Brady asked.

"Have you read the rules manual yet?" David asked.

"Uh . . ." Brady was baffled and had no idea that there was a manual of rules for eating. "I haven't gotten to that yet . . ." he confessed.

"The first rule in the book says, if the girls and boys are on different sides of the cafeteria, you're not allowed to go over without special permission."

"Oh."

"If you're going to get to your sister, then you're going to need a plan to get you into the girls' dorms."

"Me? Why not all of us?"

"Why not, David? It could be fun sneaking into uncharted territory," Andrew convinced David.

"Fun, like how?"

"Uh, I like sneaking into places, plus you got an A+ in stealth class, and with my excellence in planning and Brady's brilliance in technology . . ."

"Fine. I'll do it," David gave in.

After lunch, they went to their room and began visualizing a plan of attack. Andrew got out his map of the academy and began to sketch out what they would do and where they would go. Soon, they were in the hall and started the first phase of their plan.

Then the boys ran down the hall toward the girls' dorm until the white walls with blue lining changed into white walls with pinkish purple lining.

"This is it," Brady whispered to them.

"This is it," Andrew whispered. "I thought it would be more girly, but it's basically exactly the SA—" Andrew's jaw dropped.

They walked into a lobby full of cool things. There was a build-your-own-pizza bar, a spa, a lounge, and a separate practice training room for the gadgets that they had been issued.

"There is a HUGE PROBLEMO HERE. THEY HAVE *WAY* MORE STUFF THAN THE BOYS DO. HOW COME WE ONLY HAVE HALF OF THIS STUFF IN OUR LOBBY?" Andrew whisper shouted.

Brady clapped his hand over Andrew's mouth. "Dude, we have a way bigger problem than that right now. This place is CRAWLING with GIRLS."

David looked around. He saw girls walking around showing

off their new gear. Some girls were playing dress up in the disguise room, and others were headed back to their rooms from an evening out. Some of the girls were even texting on their phones while they lounged in the middle of the lobby.

Never in David's life had he seen so many girls in one place other than the mall. How was it possible for so many girls to be in one place without annoying each other?

Girls are so confusing, David thought. He shook his head and concentrated on the task at hand. "There is no way we can just walk through here without being noticed," he said.

Brady looked at Andrew, Andrew looked at David, and David looked at Brady. Then Brady looked around the room. He was confused, discouraged, and really hungry because he didn't get to finish the rest of his spaghetti. He didn't know what to do. Usually, his sis always came through in times like this, but in this situation, they seemed miles apart.

Well, what are we going to do now? Brady thought.

6

STRANGE THINGS

Brady, Andrew, and David were just about to give up on their mission when Brady had an idea. He was looking in the direction of the disguise room that was filled with wigs and other outfits. These costumes could make them look convincing enough to walk the halls without being recognized. He put his hand up in the stop position at the other boys, who were heading back toward their dorms.

"Wait," he said in a sharp tone.

Andrew looked at him in confusion. What else could they possibly do? There was no way to get into Brady's sister's room without being noticed. He thought Brady had lost his marbles.

"Come on, bro, you know there is nothing else we can do. We'll just have to give up. We're on our own."

"I did not come this far to give up and quit our mission now. I have a plan."

"And what would that be?" Andrew asked in a quizzical tone.

"See that disguise room over there?"

"Yeah, what about it?"

"If we can manage to sneak in there, then we can disguise ourselves as girls and blend in with everybody else," Brady said with confidence. He was proud of his plan and just knew it would work. Andrew looked at how far away the room was.

"How do we get to the room without being noticed?" he asked.

Brady reminded Andrew about the disappearing gadget that the academy had given them as standard issue. It was attached to everyone's belt for quick access. When activated, the gadget gives them about one minute of complete disappearance. That would give them enough time to dart across the room. Andrew had never really seen such determination before.

"Let's get to it," he said, pushing the button on his black and green belt. He suddenly disappeared into thin air. The other boys did the same and started to make their way across the lobby to the room.

Andrew bumped into several girls, trying not to blurt out, "Oops, my bad, sorry," "oh boy," or even "hello." They finally reached the disguise room and made their way in before their disappearing effect wore off and they were spotted. They hid behind a shelf full of shoes and paused to catch their breath.

Suddenly, they heard voices. The voices were getting louder and louder until the boys knew that girls were just right around the corner. Andrew and David hid in nearby hangers full of dresses. Brady was about to join them when he heard a familiar voice. He heard laughing, and not just any laugh. It was a special laugh. He would recognize that laugh anywhere.

"BRADY," Andrew whispered. The voices were right around the corner. Brady would be caught. Andrew whispered his name louder this time, "BRADY!" But Brady had already moved. Before Andrew knew it, Brady was standing in front of three girls, and not just any three girls. They were Abby, Christy, and Laci.

The girls were so stunned that they dropped what was in their hands. Abby opened her mouth wide, but nothing came out. She started to mutter words like, "B-b-boys i-in d-d-dressing-room." She shrieked. Christy covered her mouth with her hand and turned toward Brady.

"What's a boy like you doing here anyway?" she asked.

Laci stared at her brother. Brady was waiting for what she would say.

"B-Brady, what are you doing here?"

"We came to find you guys," he said.

"Came to find us?" Christy asked.

Brady motioned at Andrew and David to come over.

"Brady, what was so important that you had to sneak into the girls' dorms to tell us?" Laci asked.

"Some strange things are going on in the guys' wing. It feels like we're being watched, and the funny thing is, we are the only ones who seem to notice it. We snuck out of class to investigate and found out that someone was roaming the halls during teaching hours too."

"You're not the only ones," Laci told him. "We've been noticing the same things too, but we also found some other stuff. When we were in surveillance class, all of the screens went blank for a moment, and then there was laughing. It was a mean laugh. Not a happy one. Then out of nowhere, things were back to normal. We looked around, but the thing is, nobody—not even the professor—noticed anything strange. It was like they thought nothing had happened."

Brady rubbed his chin, deep in thought. What was happening? It might be a few electrical shortages, but that doesn't explain how they felt like someone was watching them all the time, or how nobody else was noticing anything weird. Something was wrong. Very wrong. He looked around the room, and then suddenly, there was a flash of light, then darkness. The power went out. Brady heard screams coming from girls outside the room. Laci felt around and accidentally slammed her hand into Andrew's face.

"Ouch!" he shouted.

"Oops, sorry, Andrew, but in case you haven't noticed, NOBODY CAN SEE ANYTHING."

Andrew rolled his eyes in frustration. *Why do girls always have to be sarcastic and picky, and, I don't know... annoying?* he thought. *How do my parents always get along anyway?*

"Guys, stop your bickering," Abby butted in. "Listen." They all waited, and sure enough, there was a rustling noise over the speakers.

"Hello, students of GUARD Academy," said a low, raspy voice. "You might not know who I am, but I know who you all are."

There was a pause. Everybody got quiet.

"Let's cut to the chase, shall we? I have chosen six agents in training who must decide how to stop me. The agents are: Abby Swing, Christy Haul, Andrew Brach, David Cue, Brady Danger, and Laci Danger."

Laci froze, stunned by what she just heard. *Why? Why us?*

"I have set six major catastrophes in the academy. They will go off within the next week. To prevent any of these from happening, you must figure out my riddles, find out where I have placed my traps, and prevent them from happening before the time runs out—and all your fellow agents and teachers are dead. To get your first clue, you must meet me in the Tech Lab tonight at 8:00, and no later. You might also be wondering who I am. Well, you may address me as ... 'The Assassin.'"

The speakers turned off, and the lights went back on. Just the thought of his name sent shivers down Abby's back.

"Is he really going to kill people?" she asked.

Andrew looked at her and smiled mischievously. "Oh yeah, just because his name is the Assassin doesn't mean he will kill people," he said in a babyish voice.

"For real?"

"Of course, he is going to kill people! Didn't you hear what he said?" Andrew yelled and folded his arms.

Abby's eyes filled with tears at the thought of her friends being killed, at the thought of *anyone* being killed. She knew how it felt to lose somebody, and she didn't want it to happen to her again, or to any of her friends. Andrew opened his mouth. David knew he was going to say something hurtful to Abby.

"Oh, go ahead and cry," Andrew said annoyed. "Like it will make anything be—"

"Andrew, quit it," David said as he stood in front of Abby. "Teasing and mocking somebody isn't going to make matters any better. And it really isn't helpful when you mock one of your teammates." Andrew raised one eyebrow and grinned.

"Wow, you sure are protective of that little flower there," he said, still grinning.

David's face turned cherry red, and Abby sheepishly blushed with a cute smile. David just stood there unable to move or to say anything. Abby walked up to him and smiled.

"Well, at least, I know there is someone to protect me on this mission," she said, blushing.

David's face got even redder. He tried to smile, but all that came out was a funny-looking grin. Abby giggled and pulled a strand of her blond hair out of her face. She turned to look at Laci. "So what do we do now?"

"I have absolutely no idea at all."

"Well, you think maybe we should come up with a plan?"

"No, I don't think so. I think the only thing we can do now is to wait."

7

THE TIME HAS COME

The children walked back through the halls of white and purple. Laci had told the boys they could stay in their room and hide out until it was time to go see the assassin. As they walked through the corridor, no one said a word. Brady just stared down at the floor with his hands in his pockets and his spy glasses on. Andrew walked with his arms crossed, peering out the hallway windows. The hallways seemed to go on forever, he thought. For a second, he took his eyes off of the windows and stared at Laci. *Strong*, he thought. *Ready to take on the role of leadership, and she is stylish* . . . He stopped and made a fist. No, he wasn't going to let crushes or gushy lovebird stuff get in the way of a mission. Andrew got distracted by the way Laci talked or looked at him . . . or basically everything about her. He looked over at David. He could almost see little red hearts popping up over his head while he looked at Abby. David's face was red, and he was making a stupid-looking facial expression that made Abby giggle nonstop.

Andrew was grossed out. What in the world was David even doing? Didn't he know it was time to develop a plan of attack instead of trying to impress his new lady friend?

Laci led them to a door that was white with a light blue outline. She entered the pass code, and the door opened automatically to the side. She motioned for them to come in. Brady lifted his head up and looked around. Everything was so . . . pink. He walked up to the window that had a perfect view of the city. Laci walked up beside him and put her hand on his shoulder. Suddenly, Brady's eyes filled with tears.

"Are you okay?" Laci asked.

"I don't know . . ."

"What's wrong?"

"I-I miss it, Laci. I miss all of my friends from school that I could have hung out with this summer. I miss being with Mom and Dad. I miss the smell of freshly cooked roast that Mom would make us when we got back home from a busy day. In other words, I miss home. Every time I look out a window, it makes me feel like something inside of me is missing, like everybody left me, and I'm all alone, by myself, in the dark."

He hung his head down and walked slowly over to a bed.

Laci walked over and sat down beside him.

"Look, Brady, I know it's hard. We all miss home. Don't you think that everybody here misses their family and friends back home? You are not the only one, and you don't have to be embarrassed by missing home, either. If you ever feel like that again, just tell Andrew or David. I'm sure that they'll understand."

She motioned her head toward the window where Andrew was staring with his hand on the glass as if he was trying to reach something. He made a fist; then he swiftly turned around, walking toward the bathroom. While he was walking, Brady saw something shimmering in his eyes. *Tears*, he thought to himself. He had never seen Andrew cry before.

"I guess you're right," he said. "I guess I'm not the only one. Thanks, sis."

He wrapped her in a big hug and squeezed her so tightly she couldn't breathe. Then he let go and went to talk with David.

Laci looked at her watch. They had about five hours till

they had to leave to find the assassin. The thought of that name sent shivers down her back. What if he was going to kill them, along with another group of kids? The thought of it sent ghost spiders crawling along her back. Who would do something so evil, so cruel? She thought stuff like this was only supposed to happen in the movies. Were they really supposed to stop this assassin guy? She glanced over at her brother and friends. She couldn't let anything happen to them, their teachers, kids, or the academy. It was a hard task, but she knew she wasn't alone. She was part of a team, and they all had each other's back.

Christy looked over at Laci with a worried look on her face.

Laci hadn't noticed how quiet she had been ever since the assassin had last spoken to them over the speakers. Laci walked over and sat beside her.

"What's wrong?"

"I can't stand the thought of dying."

"Everyone else feels the same way. Christy, you are one of the bravest girls I've ever met. Why have you been so quiet?" Laci asked.

Christy sighed and looked at Laci. Tears filled up in her eyes. "When I was a little girl, my dad and I were playing in the backyard. We lay down to rest for a bit, and my dad told me that he would always cherish the time we had together. He hardly ever came home because he was employed by the military. We started to play again, and then, we heard a really loud boom. My dad told me to run as fast as I could to his closet and to sit on his shoe organizer. So I did exactly what he told me to and grabbed my mom along the way. When we sat down on the shoe organizer, it flipped into a secret compartment, and my mom and I hid there until the loud booming sounds stopped completely."

Christy stopped and tried to keep from crying. She took a deep breath and continued the story.

"After we got out of the closet, we saw that our house

was almost completely destroyed. Well, the inside, anyway. I rushed outside to find my dad, but all I found was his dead body on the back porch." She started to cry as she hugged Laci.

"Wow, Christy . . . I'm so sorry. You know that now you have your friends to comfort you when you feel like this."

"I know, but I just don't want it to happen to my friends."

"I understand, but to keep that from happening, we have to complete the mission this guy gives us."

"I know."

"You okay?"

"Yeah, but I don't want to talk about this anymore, OK?"

"Sure, I understand."

Five hours had passed, and the kids were roaming the empty, silent halls. David looked around. He didn't like the quietness. It was driving him crazy. It seemed like the quiet was mocking him. What was happening? He couldn't take it anymore, so he held his breath and made a gesture with his hands spread across as far as he could and blurted, "OK, THIS IS DRIVING ME CRAZY! CAN SOMEONE PLEASE START A CONVERSATION?" They all stopped and stared at him. Finally, Abby stepped up to him and put her hand on his shoulder.

"Um, David, I know you are stressed, but there is no need to yell," she said softly and calmly.

David blushed. Abby wasn't the person he expected to do that. *She is so amazing,* he thought, but he couldn't let love get in the way of a mission. So he just smiled and looked at her. He put his hand on her shoulder, and she blushed.

"Yeah, I know, I'm just afraid of what might happen . . ." He let go of her shoulder, and she let go of his. Abby looked at Laci and nodded.

"Then let's get to it."

And with that, they were back on their way to finding the assassin. They entered a room full of large screens lining the halls. Suddenly, all the screens turned on, and a young man in his late thirties appeared. He was wearing a gray suit with a handkerchief sticking out of his pocket.

"Hello, children," he said in a deep, stern voice. "Please, make yourselves comfortable. I have a lot to discuss with you six."

The kids took their seats in front of the screens.

"What do you want with us?" Andrew demanded.

"Why, to simply test you."

"You mean this is just a test set up by the agency?" Laci asked.

"Oh, no no no. The agency has nothing to do with this test."

"Then what do you want?" Christy said, annoyed.

"Well, first of all, I want to set some ground rules before we begin your test. Rule number one: You cannot have any help from GUARD, and you may not contact the agency, nor your parents, or teachers. Rule number two: you may only share information among yourselves, not any of the other students. And rule number three: the six of you will call me by another name. A name that I much more prefer. Other people know me as the Assassin, and it must stay that way, but you six may call me 'Agent O' or 'Rogue O.'"

"And what does this O stand for?" Brady asked.

"It stands for 'Outcast,'" said Rogue O. "Now, here is the riddle.

"Hidden in a secret place, the answer lies. In a nook or cranny, shelf or page, another one will be nearby. Follow the clues that tell you where to go, and you will have beaten me . . . for now. You have six days to figure it out and stop me. Good luck."

The screen went blank. The kids left the room puzzled by the riddle. What could it have meant? A secret place? Follow the clues?

The thought of it was hurting Andrew's brain.

"Hey, guys, maybe we should establish a designated central

place to meet. You know, because of the separate quarters between genders."

"Good idea, Andrew. I'm thinking the library. Both genders are welcome there," said Laci.

"Cool, so . . . three tomorrow? We'll all meet up there."

"Sounds good," said Brady. "So that means we should be heading back to our dorms."

And with that, the boys waved good-bye and started running down the halls. David stopped for a moment. He turned around, and Abby was still there staring back at him.

"Bye, Abby, see you tomorrow," he whisper-shouted.

Abby smiled and waved. Then they both ran to catch up with their teammates.

8

Secrets

Christy lay on her bed staring at the ceiling. She was afraid of the riddle and what it could mean. Secret places, follow the clues, what did it all mean? She kept playing back the riddle in her head until her head hurt.

The other girls had fallen asleep, and she continued to stare at the ceiling, eyes open, wide awake. Finally, she couldn't take it anymore. Christy jumped out of bed, put on her sneakers, and walked out of their dorm room in the direction of the library. It was only eight thirty, but the majority of the girls in their dorms were already asleep. She entered the library and began sniffing around for anything interesting that might be a clue. After roaming all through the library, she noticed an interesting mystery book that had been left on the floor. She reached down to pick it up. Upon arising to her full standing position, she felt her right foot nudge something. Just then, she heard a clicking sound, then another, then another, then another. Then, the bookshelf in front of her swung open. Startled and amazed, Christy watched as the opening revealed a downward stepping stairway.

"Wow," she gasped and took a few steps backward. After she regained her composure, she started walking down the candle-lit hallway of stairs. She was going ever so slowly to take in any sound or movement that might be dangerous. Then she heard a noise, like movement; someone else was in the hallway, and whoever it was, was coming *up* the stairs. Christy turned and raced back up the stairs and into the library. She dropped the book on the floor of the library, and then darted down the hallway to her room. She jumped in bed, pulled the covers up over her head, and thought about the events she had just witnessed. Christy shivered with goose bumps and vowed to tell the others what had happened first thing in the morning.

The next morning, the girls all woke up and got ready for their first class, Stealth. Christy wasted no time telling the others what happened in the library the night before.

"Um, girls, I need to tell you something—something very important."

"What's up?" Laci asked. She wanted all the team to be on the same page and know everything that was going on.

"Well, last night when everyone was asleep, I snuck into the library to look for any possible clues that might help us figure out what Agent O could have meant by his riddle."

"And you didn't think of waking us up or telling us you were going?" Laci asked, a little annoyed.

Christy paused. She really didn't think about the others when she went to the library.

"Um, that's not the point. The thing is, while I was picking up a book, my foot hit something, and a secret passageway opened up. I started walking down a stairway when I heard something or someone and was frightened. I raced back up the stairs and into the library, and then ran to my room."

Laci thought for a moment. "Christy, that's it. That's what Agent O meant by 'Hidden in a secret place you'll find the next clue just fine.'"

The two girls clapped for Christy and gave her a big hug.

"Girls, we have to tell the boys about this before school starts this morning." Laci got out her phone and dialed Brady's number.

Brady answered his phone, and Laci turned on the speaker. "Hello."

"Brady, so glad you picked up."

"Yeah, well, make it quick; we're late for class."

"Well, sorry, bro, you're just going to have to skip your first class of the day."

Suddenly, she heard Andrew's voice. "And why would we do that?" he sounded a little cranky.

Brady took over the phone again. "Sorry, girls, Andrew woke up on the wrong side of the bed this morning. So, what's up?"

"We need to meet in the library this morning instead of going to our first classes," Laci said. "Christy discovered something, and we believe it might be the answer to Agent O's first clue."

"Oh, wow, we'll meet you there right away." They hung up the phone and headed for the library. The girls were practically running through the halls, but their enthusiasm soon stopped. They were halted by the whispering and glaring from other girls in the hallways. Abby walked up to one of the girls.

"Um, beg your pardon, but what's so secretive?"

"Haven't you heard? Some crazy kids have planted a bomb in the facility."

"Oh my gosh, that's horrible. Do you know who?"

"Yeah, six kids named Abby, Laci, Christy, Andrew, David, and Brady. Do you know who they are? In fact, you kind of look like one of those kids."

Abby had a lump in her throat. They hadn't planted a bomb anywhere. They *wouldn't* plant a bomb anywhere. They were here to stop a bomb from exploding. Abby was at a loss for words, so she backed away from the girl. She went up to Laci and said, "We need to run—now."

Laci nodded her head, and they bolted down the hallway to the library. Abby turned and saw the girl racing behind them.

"HEY, STOP, YOU BOMBERS!" she yelled at them.

Once they got into the library, the girls slammed the door behind them and paused to catch their breath. Abby was lightheaded, and her legs were tingling. They were all exhausted from running so fast to escape the rest of the schoolgirls.

"WHOA, uh, what's going on?" David shouted.

Abby was falling to the floor, and he ran to catch her.

"Somebody get her some water, quick."

There was a loud banging at the door.

"You can't hide in there forever, you criminals. I'll report you to the head guard."

"We need to hurry, now!" David yelled.

"Well, OK, lover boy," Andrew teased, "and then I'll get a glass slipper for you to tell her to try on."

"Andrew, this isn't the time to tease anyone. Seriously, she is wheezing really badly."

"Fine."

Andrew rushed out the door, bumping into a girl that almost whacked him on the head with her phone.

"Hey, you're one of those bomber kids, aren't you?"

"Uh, no, and I'm really late for class, which reminds me, shouldn't *you* be in class?"

Then he bolted down the hallway, and within seconds, he came back with a glass of water. He didn't see any sign of the girl, which was good. He saw Abby in a library chair. She was either passed out or having a really hard time keeping her eyes open.

"Here, give it to me," Brady said.

Andrew hesitated, "You sure you know what you're doing, bro?"

"Positive." Andrew gave the glass to Brady, and Brady splashed some water on her face. A few seconds passed, and then she woke up, gagging.

"Where-what-how-what happened-to-me?" she asked, gasping for air. She could barely breathe. Abby felt her heart beating through her chest. It hurt. She tried to scream, but nothing came out. David put a hand on her shoulder and said, "Whoa, calm down, Abby. You just burst into the library out of breath and fainted. Your eyes rolled behind your head, and you couldn't breathe or move."

"W-why are we in the l-library?" she asked, still having trouble breathing.

"Christy found a clue, remember?"

"Oh, yeah, now I remember."

"Uh, Abby, any idea why all of that happened? You know, the difficulty breathing and blacking out part," Brady asked her. He wondered if they would have to look out for that in the future.

"Well, I've never had an episode like that before, but I think I just had an asthma attack." All of the kids stared at her.

"When I was a little bit younger, my doctor diagnosed me with a special kind of asthma. I can't remember the name, but he said that I would rarely ever get severe asthma attacks."

The kids were intrigued, even Christy, who knew almost everything about her.

"Um, enough of that. We need to find that clue." Christy stopped staring at her and gave her a comforting smile.

"Come on, gang, let's go find some clues," she said with an enthusiastic attitude.

She helped Abby back on her feet and led them to the spot where she found the secret stairway. "Well, last night, I didn't know exactly what I hit to make the wall open up, so this might take a while."

The team scattered around the perimeter, looking for clues.

"Hey, guys," Laci called, "I think I found something."

"What is it?" Brady yelled as he ran up behind his sister to get a closer look.

"Remember when Rogue O told us the riddle?"

"Yeah."

"Well, let me replay it for you. Hidden in a secret place, the answer lies. In a nook or cranny, shelf or page, another one will be nearby. Follow the clues that tell you where to go, and you will have beaten me . . . for now."

"What I want to know is, what does he mean by 'for now'? Do you think he has another bomb planted in the academy that he didn't tell us about?" Andrew asked.

"That's not the point, Andrew. The thing is, we need to pay more attention to the beginning of the riddle. Christy, where did you stand when you discovered the secret?"

Christy walked her over to the place. Laci soon found a book on the bottom bookshelf, stuck in a well concealed cranny. She tugged on the book, and one of the shelves moved and opened a doorway to stairs.

"That was part of the riddle," Brady shouted. "This must be where the first clue is."

"Awesome. Let's go down and see where it leads," Abby said.

She was still a little woozy from the asthma attack. The gang cautiously started down the torch-lit stairway. After what felt like an hour, they reached a hallway that looked similar to the halls on ground level except that there were no lockers.

"Looks like this might have been a part of the academy at one time," David said, amazed. "It must be abandoned."

"But, when I came down here last night, I heard someone down there," said Christy, confused. "Maybe it was abandoned, and the agency is using it as some ancient archive or something."

"Maybe, but that doesn't explain why it wouldn't be at the agency, or why would they conceal an archive here."

"Maybe to learn the backgrounds and information about the trainees who go here," said Laci.

"Yeah," Brady continued, "but why on earth would someone want to learn about our lives?"

"How do you think the Rogue O found out we even went here?"

"Good point."

They made their way down the dimly lit hallway and stood in front of a locked doorway. Suddenly, there was a blue scanner light that passed across their bodies.

"What just happened?" Andrew asked quizzically. He really needed some rest. He was confused, tired, and worn out from walking down all of those stairs.

"I think we just got body scanned," Brady answered.

The scanner turned a bright green.

"Access granted. You may enter," it said.

The door opened and revealed an archive. The labels read *Spy Kid Info*. Another read, *Spy Info,* and another one read *Rogues*. The kids went straight toward the Rogues archive. The room wasn't very big. It had a huge screen in front of the whole room, along with three or four rows of information on Rogue agents.

"Brady, search up Rogue Outcast. We'll start looking there," Laci told her bro.

"On it, sis."

Brady ran over to the screen and searched up the name. A robot hand came out of the ceiling and gave Brady a folder that looked almost empty.

"This should tell us all we need to know about the Rogue," he said. He opened it up and was so surprised he almost dropped the folder.

"WHAT? Why does this folder only have one sheet of paper?"

"WHAT?" they all yelled.

"Well, it says that he has an obsession with bombs, hates kids, and he was thrown out of the organization for attempting murder on . . ." his voice trailed off. "No wonder he's after us."

"What, what's wrong, Brady?" Laci asked in a panic.

"Apparently, all of our parents were good friends with this guy, but one day, all of our parents received the award to be stationed at the Maryland location, which is the lead location. The Rogue didn't get in and betrayed the agency. He attempted to murder all of our parents but was captured by the head of the agency. He vowed to get his revenge by doing something they wouldn't know about."

"He's putting his plan in motion by putting *us* all in the middle of it."

"Guys, something tells me the clue might not be here," Andrew said.

"Where do you think it is, then?" Christy asked.

"I think it might be in our information folders."

The kids ran toward the door, but when they opened it, they discovered the head of the academy staring down at them, and she did not look happy.

9

TROUBLE

"What are you children doing here? This is a restricted, off-limits area. You shouldn't be here. You need to be in class."

The gang stared at her, thinking of what they could do.

We don't have time for this, Andrew thought. *We only have five days to figure this riddle thing out, disarm a bomb, and get rid of this Rogue guy before he can cause any harm to us or our parents. If she throws us out of here, who knows when we can return and find the next clue?*

Andrew saw Brady turn to Laci, and Laci turn to Brady. They both nodded their heads at each other. What were they up to? Laci made herself look pitiful and sorry.

"We're sorry, Mistress. I was looking in a stack of books and grabbed one, then suddenly, one of the shelves opened up. We decided to explore what was down here and find out what it meant. When we realized that it was an archive, we wanted to discover more history on our parents," she said.

The headmistress softened just a little but didn't say anything. So Brady continued.

"We must have taken a wrong turn and ended up in the Rogue's section. Um, do you think maybe we could stay down here just a little while longer, so we can uncover some details on our parents?"

They waited for her response. She finally nodded her head and led them to another archive.

Andrew leaned toward Brady and said, "Nice going, but we need to go to the trainee archives, not this one," he whispered.

"Dang it," Brady groaned and slapped his face. "Sorry, bro, I did the best I could; no turning back now."

"Maybe I can convince her to let me go and look."

"Good idea, and we'll look in here just in case there are more clues."

They both nodded their heads, and Andrew went toward the headmistress. He looked up at her. Her once happy cheerful smile and soft blue eyes that he had seen at her introduction had changed. She now had stone-cold eyes and a mean expression. Andrew was afraid that this might not be the same lady they had met at the beginning of the year.

"Um . . . Headmistress, I wasn't really looking for my parents' files, but a file of one of my friends who used to come here. He was very secretive, you know; I always thought he was hiding something. Um . . . may I take a look?" He flashed that signature smile of his at the headmistress, hoping she would permit him to go.

"You know, sometimes you can be secretive too, Mister Brach. Almost feels like you don't really belong here. Feels like you belong somewhere other than a spy academy. It feels as though every time you kids talk to me, you're lying. Are you sure the six of you are not hiding something?"

She stared at Andrew with those cold eyes. How could this warm and friendly woman they had met just a few months ago accuse them of such a thing—even though it was true? Andrew stared back at her.

"Are you sure *you* are not hiding something?" he asked.

The headmistress looked shocked and quickly straightened up as she looked at a guard that was with her.

"Please accompany this young man to the children's archive and make sure that you keep a close eye on him."

The guard and Andrew headed toward the door. While they were walking, Andrew saw the mistress staring coldly at him.

"She is *definitely* hiding something," he told himself as soon as the door closed behind them.

The guard led him to the archive which was filled with rows and rows of shelves holding information about all the kids that had attended the academy. Andrew went straight to the large computer screen at the front of the room. He knew just where to start.

"The Danger twins . . ." he said quietly to himself.

The computer pulled up a file with both of the twins' information in it. Andrew opened the file, and the first thing he saw was a picture of them together, which must have been taken on school picture day. But then he saw something that caught his eye. It was a blue piece of paper that had the agency's symbol on it (a globe with two swords crossing each other in the middle of it). He flipped the piece of paper over and found a riddle on the back, a clue, if you will. Andrew quickly stuffed the piece of paper inside his pocket. He flipped through the file looking to find anything interesting, just out of curiosity. Then he found a picture of their happy family and a torn newspaper article below. It read.

Once A Happy Family, Now Devastated

"The Danger family was a happy family just like any other, until just two days ago when the father of Laci and Brady Danger, and the husband of Lucy Danger, was murdered. Lucy said she found her husband's body lying on the driveway with an arrow stuck through his back. 'This is truly a horrible thing,' said Lucy Danger. 'My family could not even have dreamed of something like this happening. And the worst travesty is that my children are in Dallas with family this year, so I haven't had the opportunity to tell them face to face of this horrible disaster.'"

Andrew felt like crying after reading what Laci's mom had said in the newspaper article.

"Laci and Brady don't even know that their father is dead . . ." he told himself. He looked at the date of the newspaper. That newspaper was published today, which meant that Mr. Danger was murdered two days ago. Andrew closed the file and threw it on the table. He ran toward the guard standing in the doorway.

"Hey," the guard said, "what do you think you're do—"

Just then, Andrew knocked the air out of the guard by head butting him in the gut. The guard fell over, hitting the ground with a thud, like a stone. Andrew then ran toward the others. He ran through the door and was so surprised at what he saw. He almost fell flat on his face. All of his friends were tied up with duct tape covering their mouths. Everyone had been knocked out, except Brady. He was mumbling something at Andrew through his duct taped up mouth.

"WHAT HAPPENED TO YOU GUYS?"

Brady mumbled really loud this time, but then, Andrew felt a sharp pain in his back, and everything went black.

10

IN THE DARK

Laci awoke from her sleep but couldn't remember the last time she was standing. She felt something tickling the top of her lips and tried to lift her hand to scratch it. Instead of being able to scratch herself, she couldn't even move her body. She looked around. She was tied up in ropes and had duct tape over her mouth. What was going on? She looked around the room and realized that she was in the archives, but instead of all of the lights on and bookcases full of history, there was only darkness and creepy-looking bookcases.

She wondered how long she had been out. And where is the headmistress, and the team, or even the guard? Just then, she felt her shoulder brush against something. It was Brady, who was tied up and out cold. Laci was so happy to see that her brother was OK . . . well, alive, anyway. They were definitely *not* OK.

Laci managed to stick her foot into Brady's stomach. Brady woke up abruptly, startled. Laci motioned for him to wake the rest of them up. And so Brady stuck his foot in Andrew's stomach.

Andrew woke up with a beet red face and an expression that said, "Don't do that again or you'll be sorry." His face softened a little when he saw what was happening. Despite his tied hands, he located his watch. *Yes*, he thought. *They didn't take it.* Then he felt the side of the watch for a button and pressed it.

Brady smelled something delicious that made his mouth water. Could that be barbecue? His mouth watered at the delightful aroma. He turned to see where the odor was coming from. He was disappointed that there was no barbecue, but he was happy that Andrew had discovered how to get the ropes off his hands.

Andrew felt his hands loosen from the ropes, and then untied the ropes around his legs. Once he was able to stand, he ripped off the duct tape from his mouth and was relieved that he could speak again. He turned to Laci and Brady.

"Don't worry, guys, I'll get you out. Just let me wake up the others first."

Andrew hurriedly woke up the others and untied them.

As soon as he was free, Brady immediately charged for the door.

"WAIT, BRADY, DON'T—" his sister yelled. But it was too late. Brady had smashed his shoulder right into the metal door, and, of course, it was locked. Brady gripped his shoulder and clenched his jaw. He hadn't felt this much pain since he was six years old and broke his leg.

"AHHH," he yelled.

Brady was in so much pain that he couldn't stand up and fell to the cement floor. He could feel the cold cement touch his lips, then his nose, then his whole face. He tried as hard as he could to keep himself from fainting or passing out again. Slowly, he turned and saw blurry visions of the ceiling and his sister and friends crowded above him. He could tell that his shoulder wasn't the only thing that he hit on that steel door. Brady could barely hear the voices of his friends, and he felt his eyelids getting heavy. So he closed his eyes and fell asleep, even though he could still feel the excruciating pain in his shoulder.

"BRADY," his sister yelled. "BRADY, ARE YOU STILL THERE?"

Brady felt her shaking him and yelling his name. He opened his eyes just enough to see his sister and nodded his head.

"Oh, THANK GOD," Laci yelled.

She told Andrew to get a first aid kit off the wall. When he brought the first aid kit back, Laci grabbed an ice pack out of it and gently placed it on her brother's forehead. Then, she grabbed some cleaning solution, bandages, and Neosporin. She poured the cleaner on his shoulder and ascertained that it was not broken but badly bruised and scratched. She put Neosporin on a bandage and placed it on his shoulder.

"You're gonna be OK, Brady. It's just badly bruised, but do me a favor and NEVER DO THAT AGAIN," she told him.

Brady nodded his head and sat up straight. "You can trust that I will never do that again," he said.

They all stood and helped him up. Christy looked at the door. It had a small dent in it from where Brady had slammed his body into it. The door was made of thick steel, and its digital lock was on the other side of it.

"Headmistress locked us in here and tied us up, but why?"

"Do you think she's working with the Rogue?" Brady asked.

"It's likely." Christy thought for a moment. "Andrew, did you find anything in the other archive?"

"I did actually, two things. One is the next clue."

Everyone cheered and high-fived one another.

"Two is that I found out a little information on your family, Laci and Brady. Your dad got shot in the back by an arrow while getting out of his car, just two days ago . . ."

Laci felt a stab of pain in her chest. It felt as though somebody had pierced her heart. Her eyes filled with tears. She couldn't even think of her father being killed. Laci looked at her brother beside her. Tears filled up in his eyes. Brady made fists and had an angry expression on his face.

"That, that evil, reckless, careless, jerk. THAT STUPID ROGUE KILLED DAD," he yelled.

Tears were streaming down his face. He had enough of getting hurt. His life had basically been a lie. He was away from his parents. He got tied up, knocked out, and locked in a room by his headmistress and now found out that his dad had been killed when he wasn't even there. He was sick of it all and was about ready for a big blowup of his emotional feelings that had swelled up inside of him for the past three months.

Laci couldn't tell if he was sad, mad, agitated, annoyed, or wanted to get his revenge. It was probably all of them. She grabbed her brother's hand.

"Brady, yes, it probably was the Rogue who killed Dad, and we are all as upset about that as you are, but please get yourself under control. We all know what revenge did to this Rogue guy, and I don't want it to happen to you. None of us do."

They all nodded in agreement.

Brady felt his face loosen from the tight, angry expression he was embracing. He loosened his clenched fists. "Sorry, I lost it there, but the Rogue killed our father, Laci. And we weren't even there to defend Dad or to comfort Mother."

"I know, Brady, and we can discuss it more when we find a way out of this room."

Brady calmed down, but he could still feel the pain and anger burning inside of him. When they found the Rogue, Brady was going to make him pay in full for killing his dad.

"Maybe the clue might help," Andrew suggested as he pulled a slip of paper from his pocket.

"Good idea, Andrew," said David.

They crowded around Andrew as he spoke the words of the clue aloud. *"Good job, you found me, and I reckon you found some other news too. Anyway, your next clue is:*

If you seek revenge, take the red path. If you wish to keep going forward, take the path of green. Remember, you only have four days left, so hurry along if you want to save your friends."

They stared at each other. Colored paths? Revenge? Only four days left?

"Wait, we have been trapped in here for a day."

"THAT'S OUTRAGEOUS," Abby screamed. She seemed to be getting really annoyed.

"That's not good," Christy said. "Now we only have four more days to find another clue, figure out this one, find out where the bomb is, defuse it, arrest this guy—and not to mention get out of here."

"Up," Andrew said.

"Up? Why up? Everything seems down to me," said Brady.

"No, look up."

Everyone looked at where Andrew was pointing. There was a large air vent that wasn't too high off of the ground.

"David, do you have your special gadget?" Andrew asked.

David nodded. He reached into a small pocket on the side of his utility belt and pulled out a gadget that looked like a small grappling hook.

"Great," Brady said, "a grappling hook is going to get us out of here."

"Not just any grappling hook. It's a grappling hook that will hold up one thousand pounds and it's travel size," David cried out excitedly.

Brady smiled. "Sweet."

They all watched as David pried the hinges off the vent door with the grappling hook. When he removed the door, Andrew discovered that the opening was wide enough to fit one teenager at a time. One by one, they climbed through the vent and were heading in the direction of the girl's room. They didn't know that was where they had to figure out their next clue . . .

11

THE ROGUE'S REVENGE

"They have been taken care of just like you asked, sir," said the headmistress.

"Excellent. Are you sure they were able to escape?" said the raspy voice of the Rogue with a smug little smile on his face.

"Yes, sir, but I do not understand why you would want them to escape in the first place."

He chuckled softly. "Ah, Jenny, I remember that you always have questions to ask. I will tell you soon enough."

"You know I will always be eternally grateful for your leadership, and I will always work beside you," she smiled.

The mistress was only twenty-four years old and had been in love with the Rogue for some time. She knew all of his plans and secrets. The Rogue was in love with her too and was younger than he looked.

"Oh, Jenny, you don't have to say 'sir' to me," he reassured her.

Jennifer ran up to his side and grabbed his hand.

"Soon, I will get my revenge on those agents who had betrayed me. Now I have their children right in the palm of my hand."

He flashed an evil, sinister sneer at Jennifer, and she smiled back. The Rogue pressed a red button on his desk.

"This will bring me one step to closer to getting my revenge."

12

Decisions

Andrew took a right at the next turn. It was getting kind of cramped in the air vent, and it seemed as though they had been crawling around trying to find their way out for hours. He took another right turn and saw what looked like the same tunnel again.

"Uh, guys, I think we're lost," said Andrew, and groans filled the vent. "But now we know to take a left."

Brady's eyes went wide. "So you're saying we've been GOING IN CIRCLES THIS WHOLE TIME?"

"WELL, IT'S KIND OF HARD TO NAVIGATE AN AIR VENT SYSTEM, AND, YEAH, THE LAST TIME I CHECKED, WE DIDN'T HAVE A MAP EITHER."

"WELL, THAT'S JUST GREAT!"

"GUYS," Christy yelled over them, and then lowered her voice to a quiet whisper, "didn't the thought ever occur to you that everyone near a vent can *hear* us?"

The guys looked at each other. "Oops," they said in unison.

Brady looked over at Andrew and smiled sheepishly. "Uh, sorry, man, just a bit upset about this whole thing."

"We all are, dude," David whispered behind him. "Remember, this Rogue is after *all* of us; we need to stop him *together*."

"Yeah, I guess you're right."

They took a left at the next turn and headed straight for a fork in the vents. The two vents had lights above them. One had a red light, and the other had a green light. Laci thought about the riddle.

"That's it, of course," she whispered.

Everyone stared at her. "What's it?" Brady asked, really confused.

"The riddle said something about lights in our path. The green one should take us where we need to go," Laci explained.

They all climbed down the green tunnel, and sure enough, there was a vent door waiting for them. It was even unscrewed. Something didn't feel right to Christy. Who leaves a vent door unscrewed and open for all to see? Something was up.

Brady pushed the vent door aside and jumped down. Everyone else followed, and everything seemed fine . . . until Laci saw her brother staring at a strange object with a clock on it.

"Uh, Brady, what is that?"

Brady mumbled something that she couldn't hear.

"Brady, are you OK?"

"THE BOMB! IT'S RIGHT HERE, AND THE ROGUE TRICKED US. WE DON'T HAVE FOUR DAYS. WE ONLY HAVE TEN MINUTES!" he shouted.

Everyone stared at him in shock.

"WHAT!" they shouted, rushing over to him and the bomb. They all watched as the clock turned from nine to eight.

"No, no, no, no, NO, NO. THIS CAN'T HAPPEN NOW, NOT NOW," Andrew yelled in frustration as he slapped his hands over his face.

Laci took charge of the situation. "Look, team, this is what we've been training for, isn't it? Let's move. Brady, you and Andrew start working on deciphering the bomb. Abby, you and David find that Rogue and teach him a lesson and also grab some gadgets on the way. Christy and I will start evacuating this part of the academy. LET'S DO IT! GO GO GO!"

Just like Laci ordered, they all went off and did their part. David, Abby, Christy, and Laci left the boys behind to disarm the bomb and started climbing around in the vents to see where to go. Abby and David went down the red-lit vent way, and Christy and Laci went down the vent way with no light at all. While climbing in the vents, Laci was thinking of many things. *What if none of this turns out OK? What if we fail? What if we all fail and lots of lives are lost, including our own, or our parents?*

She thought for a moment about how her father had died and of how this Rogue had murdered him. She remembered the time when she came back from school, crying. Her dad had sat down and asked her what was wrong. She was only in the fourth grade.

"When I went to volleyball practice, I kept falling, and these mean older girls laughed at me and called me 'clumsy foot,'" she had told him. She remembered how he looked at her with his big blue eyes and said, "Oh, Laci, ignore them; they can't hurt you. They are just trying to make themselves look cool but in a very wrong way. All you need to do is the right thing and never give up."

Those words had always stayed in her heart ever since that day. She knew she couldn't give up now. She had to do the right thing and keep on trying, just as her dad had said. *No,* she thought, *I am not going to let fear take over. I will make my father proud and do the right thing and NEVER give up!*

She turned toward Christy and said, "Are you ready?"

"As ready as I'll ever be."

Laci smiled, and they both took off the vent door and jumped out.

13

RISKY BUSINESS

David and Abby crawled through the vent system that glowed a vibrant red. Abby looked down the back of the tunnel. It seemed like the red lights were screaming at her, "Danger, get away!" She got a big lump in her throat and turned toward the front of the vent. After that, she never looked back again.

They finally reached a vent door. It was also unscrewed, but David didn't push it open. Something just didn't seem right. He quietly looked through the vent and saw the Rogue with the headmistress talking to each other in front of a giant screen. He listened to their conversation.

"Look at them," said the Rogue with a mean snarl on his face. "So full of potential, so outgoing. I must say that they impress me." He paused.

David turned his attention toward the big screen. He stared in awe as he could see Andrew and Brady on the screen, trying to defuse the bomb. He looked to the side of the screen and saw a video clip of what happened just three minutes earlier. The Rogue just kept rewinding, and rewinding, and rewinding the clip. David turned toward Abby, who looked as shocked as he was.

"He," she whispered, "he has been spying on us ever since we found the bomb."

"Does that mean he knows we're here?" A low, villainous chuckle soon answered David's question.

"Why, did you really think I was going to let you get away with this?"

David looked through the vent in search of Rogue O. He had disappeared. Suddenly, the vent door opened. The kids were jerked out of the vent and tied up. "Children," said the Rogue, "I'm impressed with your confidence that you can beat me, but it won't be that easy. See your friends there?"

He pointed to the screen that showed where the rest of the kids were. Christy and Laci were clearing the area above, and Brady and Andrew trying to defuse the bomb below.

"In exactly five minutes, that bomb will explode, and only I know the pass code to unlocking it."

Rogue O held out a slip of paper in front of David's face. *The code,* David thought, *Rogue O and the school headmistress will have to leave this room at some point, and, of course, he will leave the code behind for me to look at as everything blows. He has no idea that nothing will explode because he's too full of himself to think that there is a flaw in his plan.*

The Rogue looked at his watch.

"Speaking of time bombs, we must be on our way. And, oh, I'll leave this code here for you. I want it to be the last thing you'll ever see before you're destroyed."

They slipped behind the door, and Abby yelled, "YOU'LL NEVER GET AWAY WITH THIS, YOU MURDERER!"

The Rogue opened the door and with a smug smile on his face, said, "Oh, dear child, I already have."

He walked out the door and broke into a run for the helicopter pad.

David quickly reached for his watch. In a split second, he activated the laser and sliced through the ropes that tied up him and Abby. They raced over to the computer and David grabbed the intercom mic to alert the other team members.

"Andrew, Brady, listen very carefully," he began. "Are you working with a keypad lock?"

"Yeah, you got something?"

"Huge. It will shut the bomb down."

"Give it to us."

"OK, here we go. The code is twelve Rogues."

David wondered why the pass code was twelve Rogues. The Rogue never did anything that was not significant. The boys on the other end put in the pass code . . . and held their breath. A minute passed by, and then it happened. The bomb was defused, gone, and dead. Now, all they had to do was take care of the Rogue. The boys high-fived and fist bumped each other.

"OK, guys," Abby said, "we'll leave you to it. We've got a Rogue to catch."

Abby and David ran down the hall and raced toward the helicopter pad. David looked out a window near the helicopter pad, only to see the Rogue and the headmistress boarding the helicopter. They ran outside to the pad, but . . . too late, the helicopter had just lifted off the ground. David wasn't giving up that easily, though. He grabbed Abby's hand tightly and jumped onto the landing bars of the helicopter. And there they hung for dear life.

THE DANGERS

"Does that mean he knows we're here?" A low, villainous chuckle soon answered David's question.

"Why, did you really think I was going to let you get away with this?"

David looked through the vent in search of Rogue O. He had disappeared. Suddenly, the vent door opened. The kids were jerked out of the vent and tied up. "Children," said the Rogue, "I'm impressed with your confidence that you can beat me, but it won't be that easy. See your friends there?"

He pointed to the screen that showed where the rest of the kids were. Christy and Laci were clearing the area above, and Brady and Andrew trying to defuse the bomb below.

"In exactly five minutes, that bomb will explode, and only I know the pass code to unlocking it."

Rogue O held out a slip of paper in front of David's face. *The code,* David thought, *Rogue O and the school headmistress will have to leave this room at some point, and, of course, he will leave the code behind for me to look at as everything blows. He has no idea that nothing will explode because he's too full of himself to think that there is a flaw in his plan.*

The Rogue looked at his watch.

"Speaking of time bombs, we must be on our way. And, oh, I'll leave this code here for you. I want it to be the last thing you'll ever see before you're destroyed."

They slipped behind the door, and Abby yelled, "YOU'LL NEVER GET AWAY WITH THIS, YOU MURDERER!"

The Rogue opened the door and with a smug smile on his face, said, "Oh, dear child, I already have."

He walked out the door and broke into a run for the helicopter pad.

David quickly reached for his watch. In a split second, he activated the laser and sliced through the ropes that tied up him and Abby. They raced over to the computer and David grabbed the intercom mic to alert the other team members.

"Andrew, Brady, listen very carefully," he began. "Are you working with a keypad lock?"

"Yeah, you got something?"

"Huge. It will shut the bomb down."

"Give it to us."

"OK, here we go. The code is twelve Rogues."

David wondered why the pass code was twelve Rogues. The Rogue never did anything that was not significant. The boys on the other end put in the pass code . . . and held their breath. A minute passed by, and then it happened. The bomb was defused, gone, and dead. Now, all they had to do was take care of the Rogue. The boys high-fived and fist bumped each other.

"OK, guys," Abby said, "we'll leave you to it. We've got a Rogue to catch."

Abby and David ran down the hall and raced toward the helicopter pad. David looked out a window near the helicopter pad, only to see the Rogue and the headmistress boarding the helicopter. They ran outside to the pad, but . . . too late, the helicopter had just lifted off the ground. David wasn't giving up that easily, though. He grabbed Abby's hand tightly and jumped onto the landing bars of the helicopter. And there they hung for dear life.

14

Helicopter Chase

David firmly held to the edge of the helicopter. Abby clung to him as she dangled from his strong grip.

"WELL," Abby yelled over the loud roar of the helicopter blades, "I GUESS THIS IS THE RIGHT TIME TO SAY ANYTHING YOU WANT TO SAY BEFORE WE PLUNGE TO THE GROUND, AND, WELL . . . YOU KNOW."

David hesitated. He had been waiting to tell her for a while now, but he wasn't sure if they would be able to if they plunged to their death.

"ACTUALLY, THERE ARE SOME THINGS I WANT TO SAY, ABBY," he yelled over the loud, whirling wind. "ONE, WE AREN'T GOING TO DIE. I'LL MAKE SURE OF THAT. AND TWO, WILL YOU, UM, GO OUT WITH ME SOMETIME?"

Abby was shocked. Not only was he asking her out before they plunged to their death, but he would make sure they were both safe. Her cheeks glowed bright red.

"UM, I SHOULDN'T HAVE ASKED. NOT RIGHT NOW AT THIS TIME. JUST FORGET IT. YOU DON'T HAVE TO SAY YES," David said.

"NO, DAVID, I'LL GO WITH YOU. THIS IS JUST A STRANGE TIME TO BE ASKING," she answered.

Happiness and a little bit of confusion filled her. She felt safe and secure after David's promise of safety.

David swung his hand over, so she could grab on to the ledge. She grabbed on tightly to it and his hand. The door of the huge helicopter was open, so they climbed inside without being noticed. They crawled behind some bags and began to listen to the Rogue's conversation.

"Ah, my darling," the Rogue said sweetly. His words were like silk, instead of the raspy, tired, hateful voice that they were used to hearing, "those children are fools; obnoxious little brats. Do not worry about them. They will all be dead by the time this helicopter reaches 300 feet. Just look out the window and watch the explosion as they blow up."

Abby and David heard them move in their seats, then the sound of the door closed. *No turning back now,* David thought. There was a long pause until they heard the voice of the headmistress.

"Um, Edgar, the academy hasn't exploded yet."

"I know, I know; probably a glitch in the programming. Don't worry; it will blow any second now."

There was another long pause; then they heard voices again. "WHY," the Rogue shouted, "WHY HASN'T IT BLOWN UP YET? IT'S SUPPOSED TO BLOW UP."

This was an opportunity for David. He grabbed a Taser from his utility belt and walked up behind the Rogue. He quickly pressed the Taser up against the Rogue's neck and fired. Abby did the same with the headmistress. David called the rest of the gang on his com link.

"Andrew?"

"Yah?"

"We have run into a slight problem. Can you send backup?"

"Yes, ASAP."

Within just a matter of minutes, the head of the agency and the rest of their team came to their rescue. Guards had swung from grappling hooks into the helicopter and took over its operation. A pilot swung aboard and took over the controls. Soon, he landed the helicopter, and everyone was safe. The authorities arrested and handcuffed the Rogue and headmistress. The Rogue had recovered from the Taser shock and was giving the kids a most sinister, evil look.

"Don't get too comfortable, kids. There are still eleven more Rogues, and eleven more disasters headed your way. I am *not* through with you yet. We will all get our revenge on you and the GUARD agency," Rogue O yelled.

The kids stared back at him and watched as he was thrown into a police car and taken away to a highly guarded prison. They all looked at each other in wonder.

"What do you think he meant by all of that?" Brady asked his sis.

"I don't know, but I have a feeling that this won't be the last time we'll work together."

"Well, in that case," Andrew said with a big smile, "all in favor of Laci as team leader, please raise your hand."

Everyone raised their hand, and Laci was honored.

"Only if Brady leads with me."

She grabbed her brother and pulled him closer to her side. She ruffled his spiky blond hair. Then he saw the head of the agency heading toward them, and he quickly straightened up.

"Hello, trainees, you did a fine job of catching these criminals, defusing a bomb, working together, and you saved many lives. The agency is in your debt," he said.

The team of trainees smiled warmly.

"We couldn't have done it without each other," said Laci. "It was a team effort and everyone did a fantastic job. Everyone did their best, and that is why we were successful."

The head of the agency smiled with pride at his young group of warriors.

"Well, I would like to congratulate you, because you just graduated from trainees to Secret Agents. We will send all six of you back to New York and meet you there."

The kids looked at each other. The girls squealed with excitement, and the boys high-fived and fist bumped.

"I CAN'T BELIEVE IT. WE ARE SECRET AGENTS, AHHHHH!" Abby squealed and was jumping up and down frantically. Brady had never seen anyone so excited before in his life.

"Abby," he began, "how come you can muster up enough breath to jump like that and not be able to run down the hall from a crazy girl?"

Abby stopped jumping. She put her hand on her chin, somewhat perplexed, and thought, *Why is that the case?*

"I don't know, but I do know that we should probably start packing if we're going to make it to our plane on time."

The kids raced back to their rooms and began packing up their things. Once they had finished their packing, the group met up at the entrance of the academy, hopped into a car, and drove to the airport. They couldn't wait until graduation time came.

15

GRADUATION IN JEOPARDY

The new Secret Agents got to the airport safely under the watch of the guards. They boarded the plane and headed to New York. Brady was filled with excitement and could hardly wait to get home to see his mom and his old friends. He was excited about becoming a secret agent. But now, he was also looking forward to settling back into his old room and playing on his Xbox again. He was squeezed between Andrew and David with the girls occupying the seats in front of them. The guards were sitting beside the girls and boys during the flight.

Suddenly, the plane started shaking. They soon heard a crackle over the speakers.

"Hello, passengers, this is your captain speaking. I ask you to please buckle your seat belts. We are experiencing some mild turbulence."

Brady buckled his seat belt and grabbed the bottom of his seat. He hated turbulence and didn't even like flying in a plane on a calm day. He had seen so many movies where there was turbulence, and the plane crashed. He hated to think about that, so he tightened his grip on the seat. The plane shook even harder this time, and Brady didn't feel so safe inside the cabin anymore. There was another crackle over the loudspeakers.

"OK, not to alarm anyone, but we are experiencing some major turbulence now. Please brace yourselves for an emergency landing."

Brady felt his hands sweating under his seat. He was not going to let go, no matter what happened. He felt the plane going down. Brady looked at his best buds next to him. They both were holding on for dear life just as he was. Andrew's face turned pale. He was right next to a window but didn't dare look outside.

David looked like he was about to throw up. All three of them soon caught sight of oxygen masks dangling from the ceiling. Brady scrambled to put on his, and then held on to the seat tightly again. David and Andrew did the same. The plane was filled with a loud humming noise as it went down. Brady looked at David once more. His face was practically green.

"Are you OK, bro?" Brady mouthed.

David reached for the airsick bags and put one over his face. Brady faintly heard the sounds of gagging and felt sick himself.

Andrew tapped Brady's shoulder. "DON'T LOOK OR IT WILL BE THE SAME FOR YOU. TRUST ME, YOU DON'T WANT WHAT HE'S DOING," he yelled.

Brady turned away from David. Whatever Andrew was talking about, he didn't want any part of it.

Brady looked out the window of the plane, and for a moment, it looked peaceful. He saw a huge lake below that sparkled a beautiful sapphire-blue color. A small part of the lake formed a cove with rocks around it, and it sparkled in the sunlight. The bright green trees were waving at them. Brady felt calm, at peace even. For some reason, he felt like everything would be OK, and they would all be all right. Brady put his arms around the other boys.

"Guys, I feel like we should pray." The boys bowed their heads, "Dear, Lord, please help us in this time of terror. Even if you choose for this plane to go down, it is your will, Lord.

THE DANGERS

Please keep all of the people on this plane safe." Brady lifted his head.

The noise had stopped. He looked out the window, only to see that they were high in the sky once again.

The captain came on over the radio.

"Please stay calm. The plane has resumed its normal flight pattern, and we are now headed back to New York."

Andrew breathed a sigh of relief and thanked the Lord for answering their prayer.

They soon landed at the New York airport, where they exited with caution and quickly made their way across the airport to the baggage claim. After about two minutes of standing there, Abby recognized the girl from the academy that chased after them and called them bombers. How could Abby forget her? But the question was, why is she here? The girl caught sight of Abby and stared her down. She grabbed a silver object out of her pocket and held it in her hand. Abby immediately knew they were in danger. The girl, who had seemed harmless, was now holding a gun. Abby was the last one to grab her bags and started making a run for the exit.

"RUN AWAY!" she yelled at her teammates.

They all charged toward the door. Abby looked behind her, and the girl was still running after them and pointing a gun straight at them, or so it seemed.

"RUN NOW—GO GO GO!" Abby told the others.

They ran until they got to the car that would take them to the awards ceremony. The gang barely escaped, and now, there was no sign of the girl. This made Abby very suspicious.

"Guys, I don't think this battle is over yet. You remember that girl, right?"

"How could I forget?" Christy said, putting an arm around her best friend, "and now she came at us with a gun." She shook her head, "People these days."

"Could she be working for the Rogue?" Brady suggested.

"Maybe," said Andrew, deep in thought.

Why would this young girl want to kill them? And why is she so obsessed with thinking that they were bad? He slouched back in his seat. "I never knew being a Secret Agent could be so stressful. Seems like everybody is after you."

"Yeah, well, nobody said it was going to be easy," Christy replied. "Remember, we didn't have a choice, but our job is keeping people safe."

She elbowed Andrew, and he grinned.

"Yeah, guess you're right." Brady looked at his sister. Either she was in a daze or off in la-la land. Her thoughts were spinning like gears in a grandfather clock. He waved his hand over Laci's face.

"Um, hello, Earth to Laci, you mind sharing what's in that preoccupied mind of yours?"

Laci looked up; everybody was staring at her.

"What? Um . . . Oh, no no no, that's OK, really. I was just thinking about something else." She smiled shyly and shooed her hand at them.

Definitely in la-la land, Brady thought as he shook his head.

"Sis, we need all of you here now, including your brain, please," he said as he folded his arms across his chest.

"Uh, sorry. Back to the point. We need to stop that girl before she decides to do any more damage. Even if we have to skip our graduation, the lives of other people come first."

16

MALCI

The gang stopped at a community park close by the agency's base. Andrew didn't know why they were in a local park, but he didn't want to question Laci's strategy skills. As soon as the group had discussed their plan of attack, Laci told the taxi driver to stop, and they all got out. Now they were all in a park with no information on when this girl would strike next.

"Um, what are we doing here exactly?" Andrew asked.

"This is where that girl will find us," Laci said in a hush-hush, secretive voice. She had some sort of weapon or gadget gripped tightly in her hand.

"But how can you be so su—"

Just then, the sound of a gun being fired filled the air. Andrew turned around, and there stood the girl who had been trying to kill them. She had long, brown hair and was dressed in black. Her cold emerald-green eyes stared at the six young agents that she planned to kill. She would destroy them all. After what they had done to Rogue O, she would get her revenge.

Brady had enough of this girl and wanted some answers.

"Who are you, and why are you after us?" he asked in a loud voice.

"Me?" she said with a high-pitched tone in her voice. "Why, you can call me your greatest threat."

"I MEANT A REAL NAME!" Brady said, frustrated.

"Fine, you may call me Malci."

"And why are you trying to kill us?"

Malci just smiled and stared. There was a long silence, then, she said, "To get my revenge."

"FOR WHAT? WHAT DID WE DO TO YOU?" Brady was so mad now that his face was pulsating red. People trying to kill them, wanting revenge? Revenge for what? What could they have possibly done to this Malci to make her want to kill them?

"What did you do?" she said with a little laugh. "WHAT DID YOU DO?" she yelled this time.

Rage filled her. Did they not know what they did? She didn't have time for their little games. These were the chosen ones. They were the only ones who could stop the twelve Rogues, and they've already stopped one—her father and her soon-to-be stepmother. They were already in jail and probably just days away from the death penalty. She was now in charge of her father's operations. She had eleven Rogues left, a fleet of military-trained men, and smarty-pants nerds to hack into any system she wanted. She was in charge of all of it, and to kick it all off, she would kill the stupid kids who were responsible for the capture and downfall of her father and future stepmother.

"You-you took my parents away from me, and now you will pay for it."

Brady was shocked. "We killed your father? More like he almost killed us! We just sent him to prison."

Laci and the others just stood in the background, watching Brady and Malci argue about power and other things. It almost reminded Laci of sibling fights, just a lot more deadly and with dangerous weapons like guns and Tasers. She looked at the others, who just stared at her as if to say, *Hey, aren't you in charge? Shouldn't you be out there telling us what to do and how to finish this?* Laci shook her head at them and turned toward her brother.

"We don't have time for this. She can't shoot. There are hundreds of people around." Laci said. Brady turned toward Malci, smiled and said, "So, Malci, unless you want to start a riot, I'd say you'll have to catch us first if you want us dead. Oh, and don't get me started on how you handle that gun. You don't even know how to load it properly."

The gang started running toward downtown where they would find the agency headquarters.

Malci, on the other hand, was trying to figure out why her gun wasn't shooting anything. She had come alone, so no one was there to help her. She threw the gun down in frustration, unable to catch up with the young agents. *I'll get you when you least expect it; when the time is right,* she thought. She headed back the way she came, completely embracing control of what she now was in charge of.

17

ACCELERATION

Laci, Andrew, Brady, Christy, Abby, and David all raced down the sidewalk until they finally reached the historic downtown of the city. They walked inside of a small building that looked like a post office. David started walking up to a woman behind a desk when Andrew grabbed him by the shoulder.

"What are you doing? Are you going to ask her for directions or something?" he spoke in a whisper so the woman couldn't hear.

"Well, sort of."

"What are you going to ask her—directions to the nearest secret agency?"

"Just trust me, OK?"

He walked up to the woman and pulled his agency trainee identification badge out of his pocket. Andrew thought he was crazy. He was basically giving away all of their information, their identities, and the cover of GUARD. But David had never let them down before, so why should he not be trusted now? David showed his ID to the woman.

"You know who we are." David smiled and said. The young lady smiled back. She looked around the room to see no one else. "You know what to do." she said, as she glanced back at the rest of them and nodded.

THE DANGERS

"Welcome, trainees. Congratulations for making it to headquarters." She walked toward a wall and started tapping numbers on a keypad. "By the way, my name is Phoebe, and I will be working with you guys. I'm only three years older."

The wall opened up to a dark hallway that was lit by lights lining the floor.

"Welcome to GUARD."

They walked down the hallway into a giant room with high-tech computer screens, coffee stations, station quarters, all in one giant, open room.

"This is the A Facility, where your ceremony will take place. Your real quarters and manning stations are all in the K Facility."

They walked into a hallway that ended with automatic doors that had transparent letters that read KF. Phoebe swiped her ID card, and the doors opened to a room even larger than the first one. Never before had Andrew ever seen anything so beautiful and awesome in his life. His mouth started watering as they walked by a build-your-own pizza dispenser. Oh, the possibilities . . . And were those robots zooming through the air? Suddenly, all of Andrew's attention was focused on one thing. He stopped walking and caught the attention of the others.

"Dude, what's up? We have to keep going, or we could be late." Brady started waving a hand in front of Andrew's face, "HELLO? ANYBODY THERE?" He turned his head in the direction of Andrew's stare, and then he saw hover boards flying up above them. It was the coolest thing Brady had ever seen in his life.

"DO WE GET ONE OF THOSE?" Andrew finally sputtered.

Phoebe giggled. "Only if you want one."

"YES!" Andrew punched the air in excitement. Now, all he needed was a cool ride to go along with all of his spy gear.

The group laughed for a short time until they entered another hallway with the same doors as the ones before, except this one said RK9F. The letters seemed familiar to Laci as if she had seen them before. The doors opened, and Laci's answer was given when a young German shepherd leaped out and pounced on her. She fell back onto the floor and was licked by her beautiful and soft attacker.

"Oh, Ginger, these are the new trainees. Treat them with respect," Phoebe said to the dog.

Laci started to stroke the pup's fur. "Aw, it's OK. She didn't mean to topple me over."

The pup grinned kind of funny like and said, "No, really, girl, I should treat new trainees, such as myself, with a bit more respect. I was just so excited, but thanks for liking my, well, um, surprise welcome."

Laci's jaw dropped as she struggled to her feet.

"Um, since when do dogs talk?" Christy shouted in surprise.

"Since when do teenagers walk?" Ginger said in a sassy tone.

Phoebe giggled.

"This is Ginger, your robotic K9 spy companion, and she too is a trainee."

And with that Ginger did a little twirl and said, "At your service."

Abby and Christy hugged each other. They've always wanted a dog of their own.

David looked down at the pup. "Great . . . another girl to join the team." All the girls glared at him with their hands on their hips.

"Well, EXCUSE you," said Abby.

David looked right at her, and his face went pale. "Uh . . . No offense. I just need to hang out with other guys, OK? I have twelve brothers. I'M NOT USED TO HAVING SO MANY GIRLS AROUND."

They all stared at him in disbelief. How could that loud voice come from quiet, calm, cool David?

"Well, we need to move on. Ginger will come with us as well."

THE DANGERS

They passed the facility of robotic K9s training and playing tug-of-war. After another hallway, they reached the ceremony. Everybody who was a secret agent working for GUARD was all in one big room, with the General of it all, right in the middle.

18

Graduation

The six teenagers, along with Ginger, walked down the red carpet that cleared the way to the podium where the General now stood. They finally made it. This was graduation. They walked up onto the stage that the podium was on and greeted the General with a full salute. Then everyone there sat down, including Laci, Brady, David, Andrew, Christy, and Abby. The General held up a medal and called out, "Andrew Brach, son of Susan and Phil Brach, please step forward." Andrew stepped forward. "Due to your bravery, smarts, kindness, and wits, you have earned this Award of Honor. This is a symbol of completion, honor, and it tells us that you are now part of this agency. Congratulations. Here is your badge."

The badge was gold and had these words engraved on it, "*Official Agent of GUARD KID Division,*" and at the bottom, it read, "*Andrew Brach, Certified Agent.*" The room roared in applause, and then everyone sat back down in their seats as the General spoke.

"Now, Andrew Brach, do you swear to protect your colleagues and citizens of the earth but in a respectful and honorable way?"

"Sir, I vow to do anything in my power to protect the citizens of this earth and my colleagues in a respectful and honorable way," Andrew said, and he and the General saluted each other, and then Andrew walked back and took his seat. He felt like punching the air in excitement and yelling YES YES YES! So he did, in his head, of course. He was having an imaginary party inside his mind, but he started to pay attention again when he was punched by Brady in the arm, who apparently was annoyed by his absentmindedness. After a playful punch to Brady's arm, he was attentive.

The General called again, "Laci Danger, daughter of Lucy, and once honored and respected Charles Danger." Everyone stood up, saluted, and the General spoke.

"Most Honored Charles Danger, may he rest in peace." Then they all sat back down as quickly as they got up. The General started speaking again.

"For your attention, bravery, and leadership, I present to you this Award of Honor. This is a symbol of completion, honor, and the sign which tells us that you are now a part of this agency. Congratulations. Here is your badge."

Again, everyone stood and clapped. Laci felt so honored, as if her father would have been proud of her. She scanned the room for her mother but couldn't find her in the sea of people in the really huge room. She wondered if her mom was proud of her too. Suddenly the applause stopped, and the General spoke again.

"Laci Danger, do you swear to protect your colleagues and the citizens of this earth, but in a respectful and honorable way?"

Laci couldn't get the all the words out of her mouth, so she said, "Yes, sir, I swear." She saluted, the General saluted back, and she sat back down. One by one, the rest of them got sworn into the agency. At the end of the ceremony, the General said, "Here are the uniforms you will wear every day while you're at the agency."

They all looked down at the uniforms. They were the exact same uniforms they wore at the academy.

"Hey, look, they're the same ones," Christy said. The others looked at her as if to say, *Uh, so?* "Hey, I'm not complaining. I love this suit." The others looked at her and had a big laugh.

"You're so funny, Christy," Abby said with a giggle. Then they turned toward the General.

"Congratulations, cadets," he said, "You are now officially agents." The room roared in applause, and now the new agents and the General walked toward the KID Division.

They heard the pounding of feet behind them and turned to find Lucy Danger just a few steps away, running proudly toward her two wonderful children. She embraced them tightly, and with tears in her eyes, she told them how proud she was of them. Brady and Laci held her warmly, and they all cried softly. She explained the consequences that led to their father's death. After a long visit, she had to leave, and the kids had to begin their new life.

The General showed them to their new offices along with their new and improved colored and legal motorbikes. And, of course, Andrew flipped out over his new blue motorbike that had tons of intriguing gadgets. The one thing he couldn't get over was that there was actually a radio on it. The General said that the bikes could go as fast as a race car, or even faster, and, of course, Andrew was ready to test that theory. So, he jumped on the vehicle, rode out to who knows where, came back into the parking lot, and did, like, a million circles.

"How are you NOT DIZZY AND SICK?" David shouted at him in surprise.

"I've done things like that before. No big deal," Andrew chuckled and smiled.

"Only you, Andrew, would do something like that." David said.They all burst into laughter along with the General.

"Well, it's getting a bit late. Maybe you should get settled. I'll leave you to it." The General gave a strong salute and headed inside the facility.

"Oh, and Miss Laci, may I remind you, you are now the

leader of this team. You get to decide the first assignment." He departed for his office inside the building. The others followed shortly after and went into Laci's new office.

"So," said Brady, "what's our first order of business?"

"I don't know. Let me check the database to see what we have." Laci walked over to the computer that was resting on her fairly large desk and started searching the database. Something caught her eye as she glanced at the right-hand corner of her screen.

"What is it, Laci?" Abby asked with concern.

"I don't know. I think someone just sent me an e-mail."

She clicked on the e-mail icon, and a video came up. It showed a girl with dark brown hair and emerald eyes. She was smirking at the camera. Laci recognized her almost immediately . . . It was Malci.

"Guys, you all might want to see this." The kids rushed to her side with surprised faces.

19

THE NEXT ASSIGNMENT

"MALCI," Brady sputtered in disbelief. "What does *she* want?"

"Let's find out."

Laci pressed the play button on the screen, and Malci began to speak. "Hello, Dangers, and other friends. I heard that you are now officially agents. Well, bravo, bravo! Excellent work. Now the REAL trouble can begin."

The six of them looked at each other in horror. *Real trouble?*

"As you probably now know, I am in charge of armies and military trained guards, but I'm not going to let *them* deal with you. Oh, no no no. I'm sending much worse. I have twelve Rogues waiting for my command. They are to come and destroy you, and they will succeed in doing so. However, one has failed."

Her father, Laci thought.

"Anyway, after they succeed in destroying you and your little agency, I will conquer the world. And there is NOTHING you can do to stop me."

The video ended with the sound of Malci's evil and sinister laugh. Laci looked at her brother and friends. Their faces were pale, and their wide-open eyes portrayed the shock they felt.

THE DANGERS

"*That's* our first assignment, to find all eleven Rogues and get rid of them," Laci said.

"But where will we find them?" Andrew asked.

"I guess they'll find us first."

"Great!"

"Hey," Laci exclaimed, "we've already taken out one of them, and we know what we're dealing with. We need to get rid of these Rogues while we can so that Malci can't win. Are you with me?"

The six newly appointed agents looked at one another, unanimously raised their hands, and shouted in unison, "Yes, we are."

Their very first mission had officially begun. They were to find and destroy the eleven Rogues.